# A GREAT & TERRIBLE REVIVAL

## A DREAD SOUTH NOVEL

## SIRIUS

THE LAUGHING MAN HOUSE PUBLISHING

A GREAT + TERRIBLE REVIVAL

Copyright © 2025 by The Laughing Man House

ISBN: 979-8-9996247-4-1

www.LMHPUB.com

Cover Design by Evangeline Gallagher

Illustrations by Shrike

Edited by Janus

Royalty-Free images sourced by Pixabay

# a Great & Terrible
# REVIVAL

To all the showman too busy stepping on each other's heads to realize you're all drowning in the same puddle of shit.

For the plaster jewelry, false smiles, and egos undeserved.
*Pourrir.*

## ALSO BY SIRIUS

*The Draonir Saga*
Uncrowned
Partitioned
Condemned

*The Draonir Saga: Iconoclasts*
Hawthorne: A Draonir Novella
The Red Star Society

*The Gentlemen Demon Series*
Swallow You Whole
Sever Your Spine

*The Wire Killers Novellas*
Birdeater

*The Dread South Series*
Rising Sun Over the Devil's Nest
Blackjack + Moonshine
Gospel of the Cuckoo
Funny Little Town
The Devil Owns Primetime

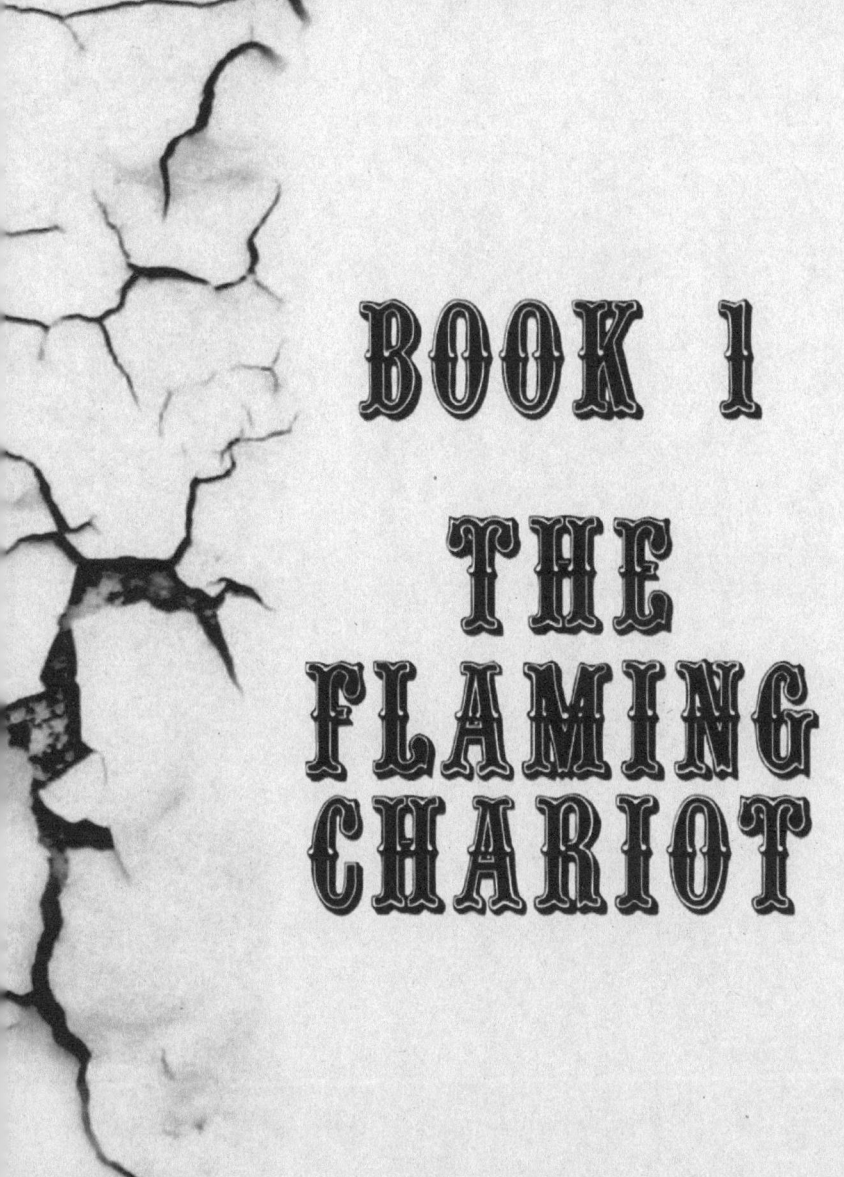

# BOOK 1

# THE
# FLAMING
# CHARIOT

# CHAPTER ONE

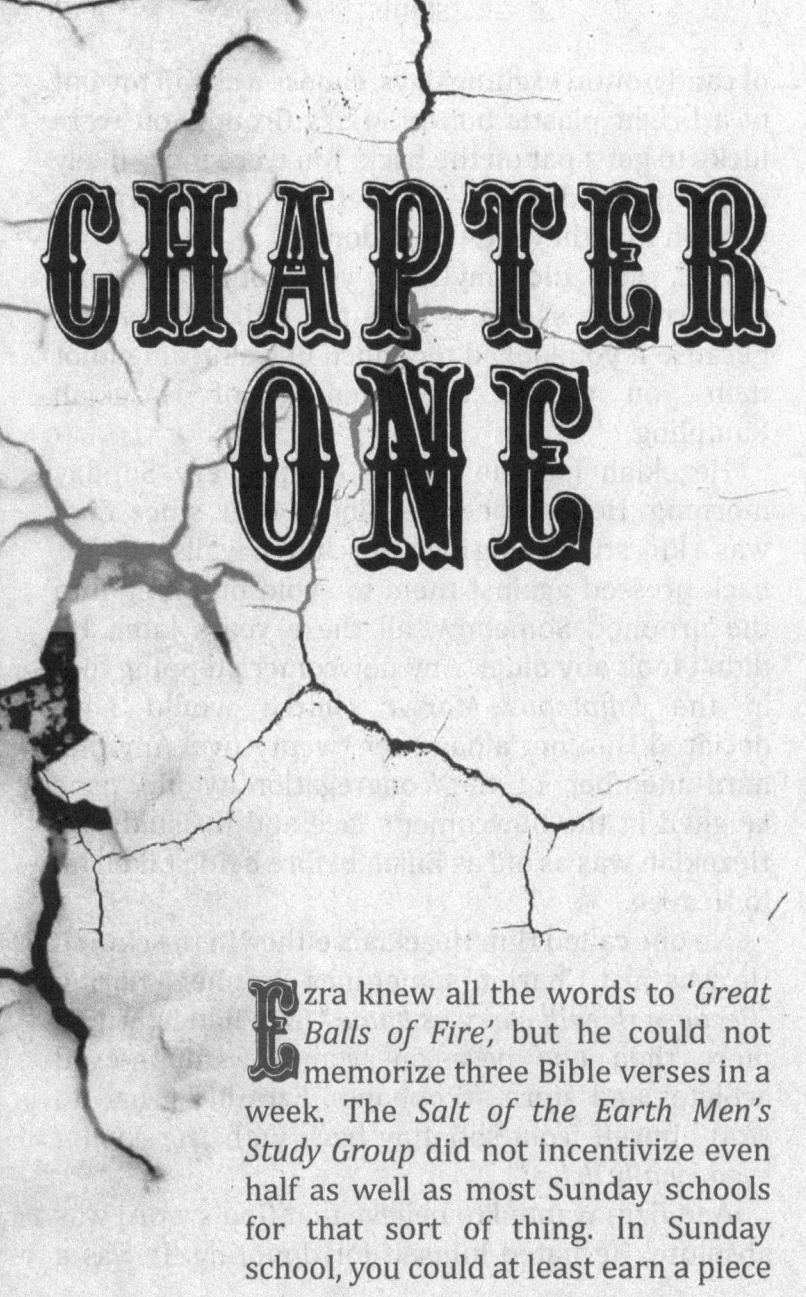

**E**zra knew all the words to '*Great Balls of Fire*', but he could not memorize three Bible verses in a week. The *Salt of the Earth Men's Study Group* did not incentivize even half as well as most Sunday schools for that sort of thing. In Sunday school, you could at least earn a piece of candy, or on exciting days, choose a cheap toy out of a bright plastic bin. In Men's Group, you were lucky to get a pat on the back. You were more likely to get a few doubtful looks if you quoted from a version that they did not endorse.

Still, you did anything you could to avoid stuttering or skipping over the bulk of a verse, because if you looked too much like a fucking idiot then you caught the attention of Hezekiah Rampling.

Hezekiah led the Men's Group every Sunday morning. He had been leading it ever since Ezra was a kid, still sliding over the church walls with his back pressed against them to avoid bumping into the prophet. Somehow, all these years later, He didn't look any older. Any newcomer stepping foot in the *Righteous Martyr* church would have declared Him not a day over twenty-five. Any die-hard member of the congregation would have laughed in the newcomer's face and insisted that Hezekiah was as old as Elijah before being taken up to Heaven.

No one called Him Hezekiah, either. In the church He was just Chariot, sometimes Prophet Chariot. *"Because He will carry us home,"* Ezra had heard on more than one occasion from the moon-eyed acolytes and stern sycophants. Ezra often had to stop himself from shooting back with *"He cannot even legally drive!"*

And Ezra wanted to believe that God's word was absolute. He hated himself for doubting. It was a heavy ball of shame that rested in the bottom of his stomach and kept him from crawling to the altar when Pastor Jerry held high his upturned palms for the call. There was a *somewhat* unfounded fear that as soon as the pastor laid hands on him, he would suck in all of Ezra's fear and doubt. He would know that Ezra was unsure of himself, a '*backslider*' as some would say. There had to be some kind of unnamed, horrible punishment for not believing that the Prophet carried the words of the Almighty in His mouth. Even if he never voiced it aloud, the thought alone had to be a sin.

*"If you think it, you believe it,"* his mother always used to say. *"If you think something hard enough, you might make it true. That is why we must always turn our thoughts towards God."*

For that reasoning, he tried as hard as he could *not* to think about it, just on the off chance that Hezekiah really did have a direct line to God, and God decided to rat on Ezra's quiet sins. There enough punishment going around, anyway, for anyone who wasn't afraid to denounce the church's Prophet.

That much had been demonstrated only three or four Sundays ago, when a woman had stood up, pointed right at Hezekiah, and screamed at the top of her lungs that He had the devil inside of Him. Carrie might have been her name, or something like that; Ezra did not know her well because she had a tendency to keep to herself. But the minute she raised her voice, five deacons flushed her out of the pews and caught her as she tried to run.

*Righteous Martyr* was a small church. So, even though Hezekiah said nothing, and Pastor Jerry kept preaching, the noise was not quite enough to drown out the sound of belts striking loose skin. Once the screaming started, the choir fired up with praise and had every member singing at the top of their lungs. It was not enough to drown out the screaming, but if Ezra pressed his fingertips against his eyelids and balanced his thumbs over his ears, he could narrow down his concentration to *just* the worship songs.

The memory was enough to start Ezra rocking back and forth in his seat. His stomach gurgled like he was about to puke, but the rocking helped. He placed his thumb against his bottom lip and nibbled at the short nail using his front teeth. The Bible with its highlighted verses sat open in front of him, along with the notecards he had made using a thick blueberry-scented marker. Ezra picked one of the notecards up and bit down harder on his nail. It made his teeth ache, but little prick of pain was preferable to the onslaught of dread he felt every time he thought about the potential of Hezekiah's disapproval.

A few more miserable seconds eked past, and Ezra set the notecard down on top of its siblings. He popped off the cap of his Blueberry marker and held it underneath his nose, breathing in the sweet,

4

sharply alcoholic scent that made him feel just lightheaded enough to not be bored senseless.

Something clattered against his window. Ezra sat bolt upright and stared at the uncovered glass while his heart was left lodged in his throat. It was dark outside. The only thing he could see was the reflection of his bedside lamp and a little bit of his desk chair. Ezra waited, unmoving, to see if the sound would come back.

Another clatter, followed by a louder, riskier clack. Ezra jumped out of his chair and all but flew over to the window, grabbing onto the sill and pressing his forehead against the glass to try and get a better look at the yard.

A hand appeared, fully lit, while knuckles bearing hard plastic rings rapped against the glass. Ezra shrieked and sprang back. His hand shook as he grabbed hold of his dresser for support.

He caught a hint of a smile, a set of almost-pearly whites that he would recognize anywhere. It was Faye Warren in a pair of snug denim shorts and a pink crop-top that showed off her brand-new bellybutton piercing. Her untamable gold curls tumbled in every which direction, almost brushing her shoulders, which was progress that she was very proud of.

He scowled at her, and she pursed her lips. She balanced the colorful balls of her septum piercing on the very top one and pressed her nose against the glass.

"Stop that!" Ezra said, making a shooing motion with his hands. Faye did not pull back. The corners of her mouth went downward, and she pointed pathetically at the window lock. Ezra rolled his eyes and smacked his hand lightly against the window, right where her breath had made a foggy spot.

"Faye," Ezra started as soon as he slid the window up. "Is there something wrong with my front door?"

"Someone might have seen me." She used the windowsill to pull herself up and swung one leg through. She slowly inched her way in by rolling onto her side until one hand was touching the floor. "And are you prepared to *face those consequences?*" She dropped her soft, cheery uptalk and pitched her voice low in her best imitation of Pastor Jerry. It brought a belly-laugh out of Ezra, even though he knew he should not think it was funny at all.

"I live alone," Ezra said. "My nearest neighbor is a chicken of mysterious origins. Who is watching you come into my house?"

"God," Faye said piously. She threw herself down onto Ezra's bed and kicked off her worn red canvas flats. "It smells like rain."

"Is that you asking if you can crash on my couch?" Ezra asked. He went back to his desk and picked up his notecards. "You have to share with Winston."

"I don't mind doing that." Faye rolled over onto her back and spread her legs wide. When she raised her head, he could only see the tip of her nose and the barest hint of her eyes. "What are you doing?"

"I am trying to get these verses memorized for tomorrow," he said. "But they're *really* lengthy this week."

"Let me see." Faye held up one hand in the air. Ezra brushed a notecard against her fingers and she snatched it up. She lowered it down until it was almost resting against her face, squinting at his handwriting.

"Where are your glasses?" Ezra suddenly remembered.

"Shh." Faye waved her hand in the air and flicked the card with a hard *'pop'.* "I am trying to learn something."

"What do you think-?"

"Shh!" Faye wobbled the card in the air and squinted at it again. "*'Thou hast asked a hard thing: nevertheless, if thou see me when I am taken from thee, it shall be so unto thee; but if not, it shall not be so.'* Hey, Ezra, not to sound stupid. But what the hell does that mean?"

"I don't know." Ezra took the notecard back and rubbed his face. "I am only supposed to memorize it, not understand it."

"Sounds like a flawless system." Faye rolled back over onto her stomach and propped her chin up on her hand. "So, are you really going to make me sleep on your couch?"

"Oh, yeah." Ezra shoved the notecards down into his pajama pants' pocket. "I'll go get some clean sheets."

"Why can't I sleep in your bed?" Faye had the biggest, brownest eyes in the world and she knew how to use them. She manipulated them almost as well as she did the soft B-cups on her chest.

Ezra clenched his jaw. He was not in the mood. "You know why," he said.

"Oh!" She huffed. "I see. We're broken up now, so I can't sleep in your bed? I have to share your broken couch with your dog?"

"My couch is not broken," Ezra said. "But if you don't like it, you can always go apologize to Pastor Jerry. He said that there would always be a room for you at the Cabinet."

The Women's Cabinet was a small building on church property that hosted twelve bunk beds, all reserved for women in the community who were down on their luck. Of course, you had to fulfill Pastor Jerry's criteria for truly *in need,* and that too deeply depended on an invisible list that existed solely in his head.

Faye said that it was like being in prison. Ezra thought that was just a bit dramatic.

"Or there is a third option," Faye said, holding the suspense for a moment before announcing, "I could die."

"Absolutely not," Ezra said. "Look, you can sleep here, but not in my bed. All right? Tomorrow you can come to church with me and—"

8

"I am *not* going to grovel for that self-righteous pig," Faye interrupted.

Ezra forced himself to take a deep breath before continuing. "—And see if you can just *talk* to him. I don't think that he wants you to grovel."

Faye snorted softly. "Where do you keep your sheets?"

"What did he *do*, Faye?" Ezra pressed.

"Nothing," she snapped. "It is not that big of a deal."

"Then why won't you apologize?"

"Because I *shouldn't have to.*" Faye slid off the bed. "He is just throwing his weight around because he knows that he can get away with it. I thought preachers were supposed to have Christ-like humility, or some shit like that."

Ezra stared at her for a long minute while he tried to collect his thoughts. On one hand, he agreed with everything she was saying. On the other hand, he knew that he should not. The inner conflict might as well have been a lead weight sitting on his tongue.

"There are clean sheets in the laundry basket in front of the dryer," he finally said. "And the pillows are—"

"Thank you." She leaned in, brushing her pillowy lips over his cheek. "I can find them."

"You'll come to church with me tomorrow?" he prompted.

"Mmm." She gave him a little peck. "I'll think about it."

# CHAPTER TWO

It started with a tremble. That was how Jerry's grandfather used to recount the story. You set your cup down on the kitchen table and saw it shiver but you didn't notice it otherwise. The tremble became part of you. It started in your soles and crept up your legs, a deep, burning itch like chiggers gnawing on your tendons. Nothing could relieve it, so you learned to live with it. Then when The Reckoning came, and split the ground open, you felt nothing but relief. Dozens of good church-going folks threw themselves to the ground and wept in gratitude before diving headfirst into the crevasse and disappearing forever.

The Dark Reverend did not feel the tremble, although he was the one who called it down from Heaven. It came in the form of tumultuous grey-green clouds like churning stomach bile and deadly funnels comprised of circling vultures.

Jerry's grandfather was one of the last people alive who could describe that day. He said that the Dark Reverend would not step foot over the city limits of Sweet Providence. He stood on the very edge with his arms outstretched and his head thrown back. He called the names of angels that did not exist anywhere in the Bible. He prophesied that God would split apart the earth and drag the entire town below the dirt for the weight of its sins like Sodom and Gomorrah.

Except Sweet Providence was still standing, and Jerry did not believe in an Old Testament God.

Jerry stood in front of his office's floor-length mirror and tugged on the edges of his blazer to button it around his middle. Having such a large mirror was a necessary evil for getting dressed on Sunday mornings after spending Saturday nights on his couch. He had no desire to take up space with his wife when they only had one bathroom, and she was being such a bitch.

Jerry grabbed his tie and straightened the knot. He wondered how much higher he would have to pull it before he cut off his own breathing.

"It's a beautiful day that the Lord has made," a familiar voice cut off his train of thought. Jerry stopped dead with his fingers curled up underneath the softest part of his chin where his thick, oily stubble stabbed him in the flesh.

"Good morning to you too, Zeke." Jerry nodded, still facing the mirror. Hezekiah Rampling hovered in his peripheral vision, lurking like a shadow born out of a night terror.

In full sunlight, Hezekiah looked wrong. Jerry found no other way to explain it, except that the prophet had a face made for rain. Sunlight only served to draw attention to His bad eye, which looked corrupted and overtaken by mold next to its soft blue neighbor. A thick, milky-white film stretched over the broken iris, with a few spots of green erupting here and there like an infection. In the very center was a glop of red, a drop of blood, that was always sliding around. At the moment, it was facing heavenward.

A muscle jumped underneath His good eye at the moniker. The whole left side of His face stayed completely still, with one side of His mouth drooping slightly downward.

12

Hezekiah clawed at His jawline, dragging ragged, blunt nails from His ear to His chin cleft and leaving red marks on His pale skin.

"There is a darkness coming," Hezekiah said. When He spoke, He overcompensated with the better working side of His mouth. "Can you smell the rain? Like gunpowder shot on the air."

Jerry forced himself to abandon his tie and turn to face the prophet. "I haven't seen nothing about rain," he said. Sweat trickled down the back of his neck, even though his office was air conditioned. He tried to ignore it. "Forecast actually predicts nothing but sunshine this week. You look awful, though. Have you slept any?"

"Better than you, I would say." Hezekiah seemed to accept the change in subject and stepped further into the office. The door was open behind Him, but His presence made it impossible to feel like escape was an option. "Did Mrs. Izzy put you on the couch again?"

Jerry drew in a resentful breath. "Married couples can sleep apart."

"Not Godly ones," Hezekiah said. He slipped two fingers down the tight collar of His dress shirt and tugged. *"And if a house be divided against itself, that house cannot stand."*

"I would rather hear about the rain," Jerry snorted. "Or whatever storm you think is on its way."

"The Dark Reverend," Hezekiah muttered without hesitation. "He comes to shake the foundations."

Something cold dropped into the pit of Jerry's stomach. He cleared his throat and tugged on his blazer again, even though the middle was already buttoned. "That's hooey," he said. "Not to offend you or anything, you're the prophet, but The Dark Reverend was an old man in 1888. My great-grandfather saw those storms. I think the only way he could come back a full century later would be if his skeleton washed up on the riverbank."

Something shifted on Hezekiah's face. His jaw clenched and the glob of red in the center of His eye dripped downward until it rested closer to the bottom.

"To question me is to question the Almighty," Hezekiah hissed. The words barely made it through His bared, clenched teeth.

Jerry tweaked his nostrils nervously and held up his hands in resignation. "I know," he said. "I know." It was easy to remember that Hezekiah was human until the words came flying from His mouth like rocks in a tumbler. Then they were jarring, and sharp, and made Jerry feel like he was one misstep away from setting off a landmine.

"Is it something I need to warn the congregation about?" Jerry asked. Suddenly, the tie around his neck felt tighter than a noose.

"Only if you want them to be warned," Hezekiah sneered. "You're the shepherd. They're your flock."

14

"Well, sheep can get mighty panicky," Jerry shot back. "So, until this man from the grave appears on my doorstep, I don't think it's fair to make anyone worry."

"Suit yourself." Hezekiah's top lip curled back on the right side, and He drew himself up to His full height. He was a head taller than Jerry, even with His tendency to keep His shoulders stooped.

Jerry pulled his handkerchief out of his pocket and used it to mop his shiny forehead. He blamed the Texas heat, and not the fact that the prophet's rotten presence made his guts feel like they were being turned inside-out.

"Church is about to start," Jerry said. His voice was a lot softer than he intended. He cleared his throat again and twisted his handkerchief up in his hand, strangling his own fingertips.

"So it is," the prophet said. He lingered for a second longer before taking a step back and then turning away. Only once he was no longer under the scrutiny of that dead, molding eye did Jerry feel like he could breathe.

The pastor wiped his forehead again and stuffed his handkerchief back down into his pocket. The prophet stepped out into the hallway and Jerry waited until He was completely gone before grabbing his Bible and leaving, as well.

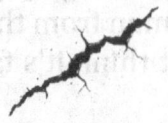

**T**he *Righteous Martyr* church had started in Frank Calhoun's living room. That was Jerry's grandfather. It had expanded since then, thanks to some generous donations, into its own grey stone building with a tall white steeple and a stained-glass window of Jesus behind the pulpit.

They had plans of expanding even more, although Jerry had never been privy to those schemes and was perfectly content with managing what he already possessed. A portrait of Frank hung in the hallway with the words 'OUR FOUNDER' engraved into a plaque underneath. There was a portrait of Jerry's father right next to it, underneath which was just his name, 'CLARK CALHOUN'. A foreboding amount of untouched plaster remained vacant beside it with room enough for one more frame. That little stretch of eggshell wall did more to remind Jerry of his own mortality than purchasing a shared plot with his wife.

He stood in front of it when he greeted people at the sanctuary doors. The ushers handed out bulletins while white-haired ladies in wide-brimmed organza hats grabbed Jerry's arm and told him how lucky they were to have him as their pastor, and how they hoped to see Isabel up there with him.

He had to keep smiling. Even though every ligament in his face felt tight enough to snap.

Ezra Buchanan was one of the last people to come limping down the hallway. His suit was too big. It looked downright comical hanging from his narrow frame, while his close-cropped hair was too limp and greasy to do anything but dangle over his pimply forehead. He leaned heavily on his crutch, and it was all that Jerry could do to keep from rolling his eyes. There were seventy-three-year-old men, and older, in the congregation who stood tall and proud. Men who never let a little arthritis or a slipped disc get them down. And then there was Ezra, barely thirty and supposedly unable to stand on his own without his knees shaking. The entire congregation had laid hands on him in prayer multiple times, and yet nothing seemed to make a difference. There was something fundamentally wrong with that boy.

And Jerry had an idea of what it was. It had to do with the way Ezra's ill-fitting suit looked ready to pop across the middle of his chest. There was only so much a sinner could do to conceal themselves, like a wolf in sheep's clothing. And Ezra wasn't fooling anyone.

It was only by Hezekiah's insistence, in fact, that he was tolerated at all.

Ezra stopped at the sanctuary doors and Jerry kept forcing his smile. He could hear his own teeth creaking as everything began to slip. He would not be able to hold onto it much longer.

"Good morning," Jerry said. He did not stick out his hand and Ezra did not try to offer his. The younger man smiled up at him, his expression reading more as nerves than anything else.

"Good morning, Pastor Jerry," Ezra said. "I was wondering if you could do me a favor."

*'Eat shit,'* was all Jerry wanted to say, but instead he nodded. "I will do my best. What can I do for you?"

"Faye is here," Ezra shifted his weight, but Jerry was no longer paying attention to him. He brought his head up and looked right past the younger man, lobbing his gaze down the hallway.

"Is she?" Jerry tried to keep his tone as neutral as possible. He squeezed the sides of his Bible, as if the textured leather pressing into his skin would calm him somehow.

"She is convinced she is not welcome here," Ezra said. He lowered his voice just a fraction. "I couldn't get her to come inside. I was wondering if you could talk to her. She thinks that you are still angry."

Jerry took a deep breath and hugged his Bible to his chest with one arm. The sick feeling had fled and was replaced by something warm and tingling. It felt an awful lot like gratification.

"Of course," Jerry said. "I will be happy to talk to her. Everyone is welcome in the house of the Lord."

Ezra's smile brightened, and he looked relieved. "Thank you," he said. "I told her that, but she doesn't believe me. I think she would rather hear it from you."

"She shall," Jerry said. He held out a hand and let it hover in the air right between Ezra's shoulder blades, although he did not actually touch the younger man. "Go find yourself a seat. I will be in there, shortly."

# CHAPTER THREE

Isabel Calhoun met the red-haired man in the parking lot of the Super Value, just like she did every Sunday. She pulled down her sun visor and slid back the plastic shielding the fingerprint-covered mirror. She bared her teeth and scrubbed any traces of red lipstick away with her finger. Jerry hated it when she wore red lipstick, so she would have to blot it away before seeing him. But her lover, with his copper-colored curls and his warm brown-sugar eyes, loved to kiss her right on the mouth until it smeared all over his.

Jonah Sweet was his name. And he did not mind a little color on his own lips. He wore Chapstick that tasted like candy apples and the taste reminded her of better days. It took her back to the brown pine-needle-covered street in Pondboat, Mississippi where she grew up. It came with memories of drawing on her canvas shoes and eating macerated blueberries at her kitchen table while counting raindrops on the window as they raced down towards the sill. He was comforting in that way, and safe. He wasn't anything like Jerry.

When Jerry kissed her, his mouth was wide and wet. He had a thick, short tongue like a slug and he liked to plunge it in her mouth and knock it against her teeth. His hands were big, which she used to think was sexy, but now she hated how they grabbed and pulled.

Isabel tried not to think about it. She scrubbed at her teeth again, trying to erase the last of the red stain from the ivory enamel.

*'Out, out damn spot!'* was what came to mind. She had auditioned to be Lady Macbeth in her high school drama class.

A blue station wagon pulled up next to a tree on the far side of the empty parking lot and came to a squealing halt. Isabel flipped her sun visor back up and forced herself to keep looking forward, staring at the dark automatic doors of the supermarket while she unlocked her car.

Thank God that the Super Value was closed on Sundays.

She didn't move, but her eyes rolled all the way into their corners as she watched Jonah get out of his car and shut the door behind him with the heel of his work boot. That station wagon was on its last legs. The passenger-side mirror was hanging on by a prayer. The headlight on the same side had a crack running through it that looked like a bolt of lightning.

He walked around to the passenger side of her Mustang and rapped his knuckles against the window. Then he bent down and smiled, and that one smile was enough to light up her entire world.

Isabel couldn't help but mirror his expression. She unlocked her doors and he slid into the car, a vision in faded denim and a white crew-neck t-shirt.

"Good morning," Isabel said. She gripped her steering wheel so tightly that the leather squeaked. Jonah's jaw worked a piece of gum, filling her car with the scent of peppermint.

"Morning, gorgeous," he said. He spoke fast. Pure Kentucky, slick and cocky.

It wasn't even nine in the morning, and the sun was already baking her inside the car. Or maybe the sweat sliding down her cleavage came from how fast her heart was beating.

She wanted to kiss him.

"We have to talk," was what came out of her mouth. It surprised her almost as much as it seemed to surprise him. His eyebrow went up and he leaned back, resting his elbow against the door.

"Are you breaking up with me?" he asked. He looked surprisingly calm, except for the frozen-scared, trapped rabbit look in his eyes.

"I ought to," she said. She leaned back in her seat as well, resting against her shoulder so she could face him. "I don't know, Jonah. I woke up with a bad feeling this morning. I had awful dreams all last night."

"Maybe you ate something that didn't agree with you," he said. He relaxed a little bit and adjusted himself in his seat. "What did you dream about?"

"I barely remember," she sighed. "It's just sort of bits and pieces now, but I remember that you were in it." She tucked a long strand of hair behind her ear. "There was a dark tree with no leaves, just naked branches all like legs on a spider. And you were dangling from it on a rope."

"It was just a dream," he soothed. He slid a little closer and put his arm around her. Isabel leaned into the embrace, stretching herself over the center console. It was not very comfortable, but she could not bring herself to care.

"I think it could mean something," she said. "My grandma and my mama both had prophetic dreams. You know that."

"I don't doubt that." Jonah pressed a kiss to her cheek. "But you've said it before yourself, dreams aren't always what they seem."

"It just *felt* so real." She rested her hand against his chest. Being close to him was soothing, as was the steady rise and fall of his breath against her palm. "Trust me, that last thing I want to do is give you up. You're all I have to live for, these days. I mean—for Christ's sake."

"That's mighty sweet of you," he teased. It was hard to be upset when his voice went-and-down in that boyish way and he nuzzled her ear where his breath would tickle her most tender spot. A shiver rolled over both Isabel's shoulders and Jonah leaned over a little farther, grabbing the handle on the side of her seat.

The back dropped, and Isabel went down with a squeal. Jonah swung his leg around and rolled over so that he was on top of her, cupping her face in his hands and smiling down like some angel.

"There, now," he said. "Do you still want me to go?"

"I never wanted you to go at all." Isabel tangled her fingers up in his curls and gripped them tight. "I just worry. I don't want anything to happen to you."

"Shh, I'm doing fine." Jonah rubbed his hand against her thigh until her skirt was bunched up high enough that he could touch the warm space between. His fingers lit her whole body up and she moaned, shoving her hands down against the back of his head to crash their lips together in a kiss.

"You *are* fine," she murmured, looking up at him in what she hoped was a demure, vixen-ish way. She pressed her hand against the seam of his pants and stroked him through the denim, gripping his hard cock through the rough fabric. "Are you going to fuck me?"

"Your wish is my command." He rolled his hips, grinding against her before pulling back long enough to unzip his pants. She worked her fingers past the teeth of his zipper and found the front of his boxers. She slipped her hand inside and pulled his cock free through the front. She liked it when he fucked her that way. She wasn't sure why.

She had never seen Jonah fully naked, but he knew how to turn every one of her dials up to eleven. Jerry, on the other hand, she had seen naked many times, and she wondered if that was why he never looked very *impressive* down below. Maybe it was all in the framing.

The leather seat stuck to her thighs while Jonah spread them apart and pulled her panties down. She had brought extra and a slip, just in case.

He kissed her as he slid inside of her, and Isabel's hips rose up to meet him. He was hot and thick inside, and Isabel wanted to cry. Not because it hurt, but because it was so, so good.

It was almost like being loved.

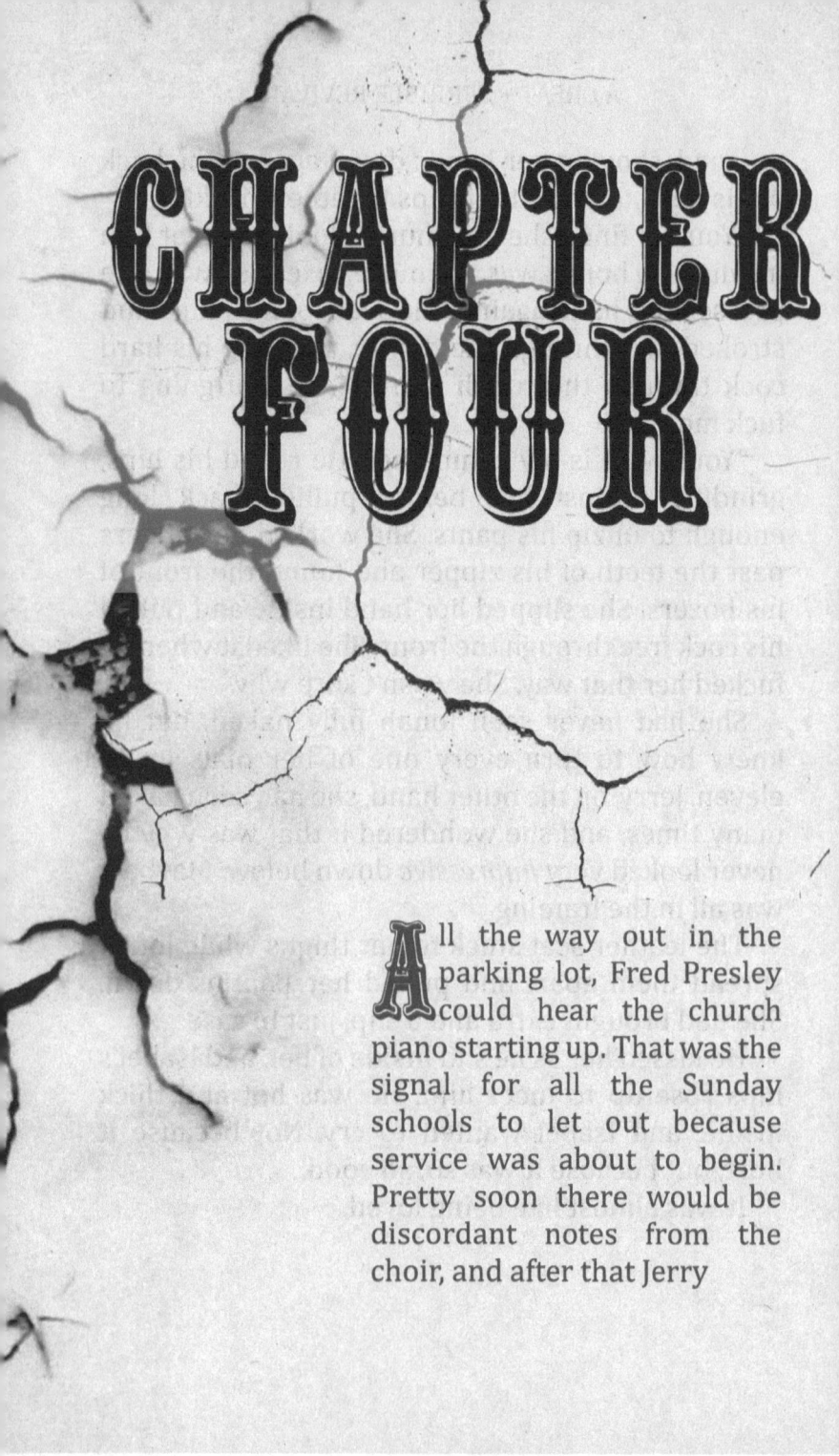

# CHAPTER FOUR

All the way out in the parking lot, Fred Presley could hear the church piano starting up. That was the signal for all the Sunday schools to let out because service was about to begin. Pretty soon there would be discordant notes from the choir, and after that Jerry

Calhoun would start his blustering—either hell and damnation or some long-winded story about catching frogs in a creek. There was very rarely any sort of sermon that fell in-between.

Fred couldn't bring himself to move from his car. The goddamn thing didn't have any air-conditioning,
so he was sweating bullets. He didn't want to crank the window down on the off chance that someone would try to talk to him. Although no one ever did. If anything, people used his car as a marker to speed up their stride. He told himself it was because he was parked so close to the door.

Had nothing to do with the eight staples in his scalp or the fact that he could not stop himself from jerking his head and shoulders at random intervals. The doctor called it a *'tic'* and said it might never go away. He did not really entertain Fred's insistence that it was one of Hell's imps that had gotten attached to his skull.

He didn't even order an x-ray, just to *see*. Once Fred had enough money he would get a second opinion.

At the thought, Fred's head jerked to the side and his whole arm twitched. He shouted and slammed his hand into the steering wheel, which made his fingers go numb for a few seconds. Fred ground his teeth and brought his hand down on the wheel again, this time purposefully setting off the car horn. The sound made the blond girl standing by the church's front doors jump, and he was able to shift his focus to her instead of his tingling fingers.

He knew her name, but he could not remember it. All he remembered was how she used to be a boy. No one else believed him about that, either, but he could *tell.* He wished that he could remember her face better, but just like all the others, it had faded into a glob of featureless skin.

The imp scratched at the inside of his skull. He could hear its talons dragging over the bone.

*'Ladyboy, ladyboy. Fly away home. What are you doing? Hey, are you paying attention to me? Hey! Hey, pay attention!'*

The imp had a voice like the villain of an old cartoon, snarly and smarmy and scratchy.

Fred drove his nails against the suture on the side of his head, hoping the sharp jab of pain would be enough to bring him back to the moment. All it really did was clear his nose and make his eyes water. He grit his teeth together until hard shards of plaque broke off onto his tongue.

The left church door swung open and Jerry Calhoun stepped out. Fred knew him because of the way he walked. Jerry had a little swing in his hips and minced his steps like he was tiptoeing over bubble wrap.

*'What a fucking pansy! Hey! That's not his wife! Get outta there, bozo!'*

Jerry reached out to touch the blond girl's arm and she pulled back. She flicked the ash from her cigarette onto him and turned away. Jerry closed the distance between them and grabbed her arm, forcing her to turn around and face him. His grip was so tight that he made her skin turn dead-flounder-fish pale.

She dug her cigarette into his wrist. Jerry hollered and the girl took off. She couldn't run across the gravel parking lot very well. Fred watched her stumble, more interested in her staggering than in Jerry shaking his whole hand and cursing.

Jerry spat on the ground and then turned around to walk back inside. Fred held his breath and silently counted to three before getting out of the car.

More heels against the gravel. Fred's head swiveled around and he covered the ugly suture with his hand. He caught sight of sensible white heels and beige stockings with twin black seams running up the wearer's calves that disappeared underneath a straight blue skirt.

He could not look up any higher than that. Once he saw the hem of a fitted blue blazer, he had to push down on his own neck to keep his head down and his eyes from wandering. The woman approached the church doors on a cloud of perfume, which sent the imp into fits.

*'Gah! Blech! Did she take a bath in it?'*

Fred scrambled to grab the door handle before the woman could reach it. He pulled it wide open while scuttling back, still hunched forward so she did not have to look at him too hard.

29

"Thank you, Brother Presley," she had a voice he would have liked to hear on the radio, crystal-clear and refreshing like a glass of cold water in August. He recognized it immediately, because Isabel Calhoun led the choir for a reason.

He wanted to beat himself up for getting in her way. He fought the sudden, violent urge to punch himself in the stomach and settled for biting the inside corner of his bottom lip. The thin flesh popped between his canines and made his whole mouth taste like pennies.

"Of course, Sister Calhoun," he said. He hated his own voice. It had not sounded right since he got released from the hospital.

He wished that he could see Isabel's face. He wanted to know if she was smiling at him. When he finally had the courage to look up, the fleshy glob of *nothing* just bobbed up and down underneath her sprayed and permed blond halo.

She walked inside, yanking all the breath out of his chest as she went. Fred leaned against the door, winded, and glanced inside where the shadows of the congregation gathered to shuffle towards the sanctuary.

He licked his lips and slipped inside, letting the door swing shut behind him. The choir had already started up a rousing chorus of *This is the Day*, and Isabel Calhoun clapped and swayed in time as she walked into the sanctuary, her voice rising above all the others who sounded like yowling alley cats in comparison.

Fred found a quiet seat in the furthest pew towards the back and claimed his place by the aisle. Prophet Chariot was already seated on the stage. He had His own avocado-green velvet wingback chair right next to the plain wooden one where Isabel usually sat during the sermons. The Prophet was the only face that Fred could still see. And He was, by any and every stretch of the description, a beautiful man. He had eyes like shards of robin's eggshells and thick, wavy hair blacker than coal. His tongue was black, too, because God had rotted it from the inside-out. His only true words, the words of the Lord, were for very few to hear, and His mouth never moved when He spoke them.

# CHAPTER FIVE

Ezra pulled at a loose thread that dangled from the seam of his black dress slacks. It spent the entire sermon waving at him, and he was finally so annoyed with it that he wrapped it around the tip of his index finger and snapped it off. Now he could roll it around between the pads of his thumb and forefinger, working up a blistering friction while he wondered where Faye had gone.

Only a small part of him had been foolish enough to believe that she would sit through an entire church sermon, but he thought she might at least try for the sake of a hot meal and a bunk bed.

Ezra pressed the rolled-up string against his mouth and slid it back-and-forth over his bottom lip. He had lost track of the sermon altogether and became hyper-focused on the deep split in the center of his chapped lip. He wasn't sure how it had got there, but he liked the sting.

"Ezra," the softest whisper followed by cold brass prodding his hand caused Ezra to look down. Mabel Calhoun was doing her best to hand him the offering plate where tens and twenties were piled gracelessly on top of the dark green velvet bottom.

"Sorry," he whispered back. He stuck a folded five-dollar-bill down the side and passed along the plate as quickly as he could manage. The usher who took it from him was Ron Abrams, the tallest man that Ezra had ever met. He was always sweaty, and his flushed face was the exact same shade of red as a county fair hot dog.

Mabel's gentle hand fluttered back to brush against his, and Ezra's heart jumped into his throat. He did his best to swallow it down and pretended to be adjusting his necktie.

"Is everything all right?" Mabel asked. She had fine, pale hair like cornsilk and she wore it pinned up with a beaded pair of hair sticks. She always smelled like brown sugar and vanilla, and she wore a russet cardigan even though it was hotter than Satan's spit outside.

"Yeah," Ezra whispered back. The last thing he wanted to do was draw the eye of the Prophet for disrupting church, but if there was a chance for him to say two words to Mabel Calhoun, he was going to take it. She was the kind of girl he would marry, if only she was also the kind of girl who would marry him.

"You're a little jumpy," she smiled and darted a glance at the pulpit before leaning back in towards him. "What's got you nervous?"

"I lost track of Faye," he admitted. Mabel's smile disappeared and she drew back her hand.

"I think I saw her go around towards the swing set." Mabel crossed her hands on top of her Bible and turned her full attention back towards the sermon. Ezra's ears burned with embarrassment, although he was not sure why.

Pastor Jerry slammed his Bible down on the pulpit and the sound went off like a shot. He grabbed the long neck of the attached microphone and dragged it towards his mouth while he leaned over like he was trying to absorb the entire pulpit into his body.

"I tell you, church," Pastor Jerry shouted even though he did not have to, "there is a *reckonin'* that is coming our way! That is coming *your* way! Where there blood of the Lamb will wash us *all* clean of our sins and we will dance, and we will shout, and will *praise the Lord* with all the saints and holy hosts of angels! Oh, Hallelujah, sweet Jesus, praise God!" He pulled back from the pulpit and wiped his face with a limp, nearly-translucent handkerchief. Several congregation members were clapping, including Mabel, as she nodded and smiled with teeth like perfectly-even rows of pearls.

Fred Presley was fidgeting in his seat. The man looked like he was trying to get up and dance along with the pastor's odd, sing-song cadence. He turned the toes of his worn black shoes in and out, going from heel-to-toe and bobbing his head along like there was a song only he could hear. His right knee jumped and raced while his hands flew everywhere, going up and down, slapping his knees and the arm of the pew where he sat at the very end. Everyone around him was doing their best to ignore him. Fred was easy to ignore until he started whooping and hollering. Too many times had he jumped up and asked to shout his testimony as if there was a soul still left in that building who had not heard it a dozen times. Pastor Jerry always gave in, but with the worn-down sort of impatience of a man who had raised three children and knew how to pick his battles.

"And the angels will come down and they will sing God's praises! And the dead will rise up from their graves! Glory be to God, Hallelujah, I want to dance and sing and be among that number, church!" Pastor Jerry paused to gulp down water from a plastic cup. Fred's tapping and drumming was getting faster. Ezra looked up at the ceiling and all he could see were bright, yellow lights sunk deep into the holes in the plaster. The angels of the Lord and their many, many eyes.

The world was too hot, too loud, and he started to feel dizzy again.

He started to shed his blazer, hoping that doing so would help, then thought better of it and slid it back up his shoulders. It was not a good chest day. He would take his chances with heatstroke.

"Hallelujah!" Jerry grabbed his Bible and slammed it against the pulpit again. Ezra winced.

"*Ha-lle-lu-jah!*" echoed the congregation.

"Praise the *la-wd*, praise the *la-wd*, thank *ya Jee-zus!*" Fred's whole head swung from side-to-side and the light cut a vicious line down the wide metal staples that kept his scalp bolted to his skull. Every time he brought his chin down it was like watching a blade flash over his head.

Ezra shoved his hand into his pocket. There wasn't anything there for him to fidget with. The best he could uncover was the discarded wrapper from a strawberry candy he ate before walking into Sunday school. He squeezed the crinkled plastic between his fingers, but it was not enough.

The all-seeing angel eyes burning above his head brought little teardrops of sweat bubbling up on his skin.

"Thank you, Jesus," Mabel Calhoun whispered next to him. Her wide blue eyes were transfixed right on the Prophet, who had barely moved for the entire service, much less spoken.

Ezra could not take it anymore. He stood up and stumbled to get out of the pew, stepping over two or three pairs of shoes before peeling down the center aisle and making a beeline for the door. He tried not to run. The relief that hit him as soon as he went through the doors and into the quiet, cool hallway was instantaneous. Ezra staggered down the hall and fell into a flowery chair, only then realizing that he had left his crutch behind.

*"Dammit."* He glanced at the doors. There was no chance he would be going back in before service was over. Then he would have to wait until most everyone had left before he stood up to get the damn thing. Some pain days were better than others, but if he dared to walk too much without it, there would undoubtedly be a 65-year-old woman with bright pink lips wearing White Diamonds perfume who would grab his arm to say something like "now, you don't really need that, do you? Look at me, I'm halfway to Heaven and I get around just fine."

Ezra hated nothing more than that pitying look from women old enough to be his grandmother. The way they shriveled up their lips and the corners of their eyes crinkled as if they were always laughing at some inside joke. He hated the way they patted him on the arm and squeezed his hand and told him how they missed when his hair was 'so long and beautiful'. Church women were time capsules for every Doubting Thomas, Backslider, and Budding Apostate. Their supernatural ability to recall every time you sang *"Jesus Loves Me"* at the age of four came at the steep price of having little-to-no awareness of the present. Most were doing well to remember where they parked.

Ezra tilted back his head and closed his eyes. He did not dare take a nap in the hallway, but he was willing to indulge in a half-second's worth of peace. Soon the piano would start up and the wailing and crying would begin, then the doors would open up and everyone would come filing out, completely dry-eyed and ready for their lunch.

But those few precious moments beforehand, where it was completely quiet except for the muffled preaching from the far end of the hall, were just for him.

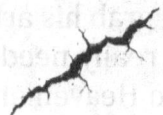

As soon as the piano music started up, Ezra heard the sanctuary doors swish open, and a pair of shoes made their way down the carpeted hall. He sat up, steeling himself for one of the ushers to come around and start ribbing him about why he had snuck out.

Except it wasn't any of the ushers, nor was it the Prophet, a terrifying prospect he had failed to consider until that moment. It was Mabel Calhoun, and she was carrying his crutch.

"There you are." Mabel flashed her pearly teeth at him. "I was hoping I could catch you." She offered him the crutch, holding onto it with both hands. "You left this behind...I assume you didn't mean to."

"No, I didn't," Ezra muttered, but smiled sheepishly in return. He took back his device and pulled it towards his side as he inched closer to the edge of the seat, preparing to stand. "Thank you."

"Of course," She glanced over her shoulder, as if she expected someone to be there. "I had to go to bathroom anyway."

"Well, I appreciate it." Ezra forced his smile to stay fixed. "Can't get very far without it."

"You should take better care of yourself." Mabel wagged a finger at him. She walked away, but instead of heading straight ahead towards the bathrooms, she veered left and quickened her pace towards her father's office.

Ezra watched her disappear. He thought about following her, but that sounded like trouble. Whatever she was up to was none of his business.

Ezra stood and started for the church doors. Through the glass, he caught a flash of Faye's bare feet around the side of the building as she launched herself from the seat of a swing.

Several small children ran to chase her. Faye tumbled through the grass and then sprang back up, running back towards the swing set with the whole swathe chasing her.

Ezra shook his head, but his smile became a little more genuine.

# CHAPTER SIX

When Baron and Duke went barreling across the kitchen tile, it always meant someone was at the back door. It was an impossible mission to stop the bluetick hounds from baying as soon as the storm door handle jiggled, so Amos did not even try.

He only paused long enough to drop the scoured pot he had been washing down into the sink and wiped his wet hands off on a thin kitchen towel. At the same time, Joel, his unfailingly flexible partner, was attempting to

hit the door handle with their shoe while balancing two armfuls of groceries.

Joel had been a mattress actor earning dazzling figures in the hidden-section VHS business before growing out their beard. They claimed to have once been able to bend their legs over their shoulders, but Amos had yet to see that happen.

Amos grabbed the dogs' collars and hauled them back long enough for Joel to step into the kitchen.

"Whew. Down, boys. *Sit.*" Amos tugged on the collars to show he meant business. Duke and Baron pulled against him, whining and swinging their tails in such rapid circles that they looked to be in danger of taking flight. Joel smiled at the hounds and laughed, setting the brown grocery bags down onto the kitchen table.

"I know, I know." Joel raised their hands and then held them out for inspective sniffs. "I was gone for so long."

"Approximately thirteen years," Amos said, releasing his hold on the hounds and straightening up.

"I should be shot." Joel pulled out a chair and sat down before Duke and Baron could knock them over. "And speaking of betrayals, is he home yet?"

Amos shook his head and started to unpack the groceries. "I hope he gets back before Zee does," he said. Joel nodded their solemn agreement.

"At least so he can shower," Joel said. "Scrub the lipstick off his neck." They pushed their hands up underneath Baron's floppy black ears and scratched. "He's not my favorite, is he Baron? No, he's not. Aww, is that the good spot?"

Amos bit the inside of his cheek, pulling at the scarred tissue that was already built-up from years of anxious shredding. "He's no one's favorite."

"Tell me about it. Even Baron thinks he's a dimwit." Joel thumped the dog's sides playfully. "*That* should tell you something, right there."

"Yes, well." Amos rolled his eyes. "It is your turn to try and talk some sense into Zee. I already tried."

"Let me guess." Joel switched over to Duke, dropping a kiss on top of the coonhound's head. "It is God's Plan."

"Something like that."

"Well, God hasn't thought too far ahead."

"You tell that to Zee." Amos shoved a milk carton into the fridge. "And then you can let me know how it goes."

A deep-throated growl from Duke brought Amos' attention back around just in time for the screen door to swing open. Jonah ducked as he stepped inside, already a tall motherfucker and even taller for the dusty brown cowboy boots he was wearing. Zee saw *something* in him, but Amos had no way of knowing what it was.

"Good morning," Joel greeted, feigning cheerfulness in a way that only they could.

"Morning." Jonah bent to hold his hands out to the dogs, which was a *choice* considering Baron was showing his teeth. "What are we having for lunch today?"

"Fried green tomatoes and biscuits," Joel said, glancing over at Amos. "With eggs, I think."

"Perfect," Jonah smiled. "Is Zee home yet?"

"No," Amos cut in. He watched Jonah's smile wither at the edges as soon as he spoke. "And you should be glad for that."

Jonah's expression shifted completely. "I'll go take a shower, then," he said. He straightened up and Joel stood as well to move out of the way, giving the dogs something to follow so that the redhead could actually get through.

"Be sure to wash your dick," Amos snorted. Jonah shot him a baleful look, but he didn't say anything in response. It was an unspoken rule that no one bucked against Amos, since he was the First and had been there the longest. It helped, too, that he was bigger and wider, and a good bit stronger. However, that was unlikely to stop Jonah from whining in Zee's ear at some other point in time.

Jonah was very keen on seizing every thread of conflict and spinning it into a yarn of disrespect. Having experienced so little victimization in his life, he was forced to manufacture his own.

"I don't think it would kill you to be nice," Joel said, although they did not sound too fussed.

44

"Probably not." Amos wasn't going to argue when he was so well-aware of his own biases. "Will you pull out the cornmeal?"

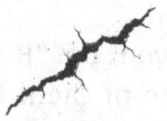

The dogs went crazy again the minute Hezekiah walked up the entrance path. Amos opened the front the door to keep them from clawing at the screen, and the two hounds went flying out so quickly that their paws did not even touch the porch steps.

"They missed you," Amos said. He spoke too quietly for his lover to hear, but he was not expecting a real response, anyway. Hezekiah sank carefully down to one knee to pet both dogs, and for a moment, Amos was reminded of years that seemed to belong to another lifetime—maybe to someone else altogether.

Before the lightning strike. Before the visions. Before the cult.

Then Hezekiah stood and brushed grey fur off the front of his suit. He looked up and Amos caught sight of that mottled, dead eye.

It put a lump in his throat bigger than a tennis ball.

"Welcome home," Amos said, raising his voice to be heard. Hezekiah climbed the porch steps, both hounds trailing faithfully at his heels.

"I was followed home by three vultures," the prophet said. He held out a hand and Amos took it on reflex, lowering his chin to kiss the silver band on Hezekiah's ring finger.

"Oh?" Amos asked.

"Yes," Hezekiah went on. "But when I stopped to cross the street, one of them froze and fell down dead without a sound. The other two descended immediately and began picking at its flesh, as if they had been waiting for the opportunity."

"What do you make of that?" Amos asked.

Hezekiah did not answer. Instead, his good eye looked straight past Amos' shoulder. "Where is Jonah?"

"He's home, so is Joel," Amos said. That tennis ball in his throat was getting bigger. If it swelled up any more, he did not think he would be able to swallow. "I made your favorite and I would love it if you ate—"

Before he could continue, Joel popped up behind him. They rested their chin on Amos' shoulder and wrapped their arms around his stomach, and their voice came from right next to his ear.

"Welcome home," they said. They squeezed Amos tightly, as if they could sense his anxiety from inside the house. "How was the service?"

"Jerry Calhoun is an idiot," Hezekiah scoffed. He extended his hand again, and Joel took hold it from underneath Amos' arm to kiss the silver ring around Hezekiah's middle finger. "He does not heed

46

my warnings and I fear he has turned his face from God altogether."

"Who could have predicted?" Joel chirped. They nuzzled Amos' ear before pulling away.

The tennis ball was too big, now, for Amos to say anything at all. He had nothing to say about Jerry, anyway. Nothing they had not all heard a dozen times.

"Amos made fried green tomatoes," Joel changed the subject. "Come eat while it's all still hot."

"I am fasting," Hezekiah reminded them, a bit of that rigid sternness creeping back into his voice. "I will not eat until the Great Revival, as God has dictated."

"The Great Revival seems a long time off," Joel said, keeping their tone as neutrally pleasant as possible. "Are you saying God would begrudge you a single biscuit?"

"Only coffee for me, thank you." Hezekiah stepped forward and Amos cleared the way, returning to the porch only long enough to call the dogs back in.

"I think he is getting worse," Joel whispered.

Amos only nodded. He shut the door behind him and cast the living room back into hazy afternoon darkness.

There was no telling when the 'Great Revival' would be upon them. Hezekiah only ever said that they would know it when it arrived. Until then, Amos was more worried about his scarecrow-thin partner, and about the storm that was already brewing right underneath Hezekiah's nose.

# CHAPTER SEVEN

Isabel loved strawberry-flavored bubblegum. It made nice, tight bubbles on the tip of her tongue and when they popped, they always sounded off louder than a pistol. Then she could really taste the sugar grains, which were her favorite part.

*Pop.*

Being a pastor's wife wasn't just a Sunday job. In fact, Mondays were the worst days when it came to catching up on the answering

machine and the line of needy new members who would be knocking on the office door.

But weren't Mondays like that for everyone?

*Pop.* She unlocked the office door with a jangling set of keys that weighed about as much as a bag of yellow cornmeal.

Jerry never came in on Monday mornings. That had only happened for the first year they were operational.

Isabel walked into the church office and flipped on the dim yellow lights. There was a stack of bills waiting on her next to an adding machine, as well as a brown zippered bag and a blank bank deposit slip which made counting the offering and dropping it into the church bank account as easy as pie. Why the deacons didn't count it the night before, she would never know. What good *were* deacons anyway, if they couldn't do that much?

It was just as well. She would never trust a man to count higher than the fingers of one hand.

The church doors had only been open for half an hour before Sarah Greenory turned up. The head of *The Women of Faith's Cabinet*, and she took her unpaid position very seriously.

Isabel was still counting twenties.

"Good morning, Sister Greenory," Isabel greeted her before she even had a chance to look up. Sarah stopped about three inches from the massive oak desk and leaned over until fine particles of Aquanet showered from her salon-made perm onto the waxed surface.

"All our beds in the Cabinet are full," Sarah said. The words squeaked out as if they were struggling to get past her teeth.

"Unfortunate, but not surprising." Isabel shoved a stack of bills into the brown deposit bag. "You know how things are this time of year, the transients, and—"

"We do *not* have room for Faye Warren." Sarah hammered her point home before Isabel could even think to counter it.

Isabel popped her gum again to buy herself some time as she calculated a response.

"Who was asking? Jerry?" *Pop.*

"Jerry doesn't *ask*, he *tells.* And he *told* me, 'make room for her, Sarah. It's what Christ would have done'. Well, I know we all strive to be Christ-like, but in this instance, Isabel, I *can't.* She's not a natural woman."

Isabel bit the barb off the tip of her tongue. "What does that mean, Sarah?"

"I am just *trying* to do my job. Guard the flock. Keep them safe." Sarah let out a gust of wind through her nostrils. "The women and girls who come to us for shelter are innocent lambs. Faye Warren is a wolf in sheep's clothing."

The analogy was so tiresome that by the end of it, Isabel's eyelids were drooping. "The Cabinet is open to everyone," she emphasized when Sarah finally stopped talking. "If Jerry wants her in, you will just have to make room."

"We don't have the space," Sarah argued. "We are out of cots."

"Find one. Make it happen. Get creative—I don't know what to tell you, Sarah. I can't argue with Jerry. Haven't had any success with it in twenty years."

"She comes through our doors spreading disease!" Sarah blurted out. "Like a locust of the end times!" Heavy silence followed her words, which were louder than a doomsday trumpet.

Isabel pushed her gum so far towards her back teeth that she nearly swallowed it. "What does that mean?" she asked. Sarah was forever pulling biblical analogies that made no damn sense out of the air. And in this case, likening Faye Warren to a locust was not amongst Isabel's favorite comparisons.

"Of course, Jerry would not have told you." Sarah clutched her chest. "I know that he wants to spare you all the sordid details of some of our more wayward members of the congregation and the grime on their souls, but in this case, I cannot keep it under wraps. I would be doing a disservice not only to you, but to every woman who relies on the Cabinet for her food and shelter during these punishing final weeks of summer heat..."

Isabel pressed her fingers against her temple, trying not to make it so obvious that there was a headache creeping its way from the back of her skull to the narrow passageways of her sinuses. With any luck, one day it would get deep enough to kill her.

"...Meanwhile, I have noticed an uptick in bumps and sores around the *intimate* areas of our residents. They cannot help but stick their hands underneath their skirts and scratch until they bleed."

Isabel frowned. "That sounds awful, and painful," she said. "Did you talk to Dr. Carswell about it?"

*"No,"* Sarah sounded mortified. "I want to spare these women the humiliation, and I don't think that the church should have to foot the bill for something so degenerate."

"Dr. Carswell has been a member of this church for fifty years," Isabel reminded her. "I think he would be more than understanding and willing to—"

"I have been treating it with my own remedy: Aquaphor and Milk of Magnesia. It's what my mother used to spread on diaper rashes, always took care of them like a charm."

"I see," Isabel folded up her deposit slip. All this talk about rashes was starting to make *her* ass itch. "What makes you think Faye is responsible for this? I have to ask."

"I found a tube of Lindane cream under her pillow last time she was with us," Sarah said. "There is no explanation for that, other than the devil having his grip between her thighs."

That imagery sent a shiver up Isabel's spine. She grabbed the brown deposit bag and everything else she needed before looking back up.

"I am sorry to interrupt you, Sarah, but I have to run to the bank before lunchtime," she said.

"Of course." Sarah took a step back. "I hope you see things from my point of view, Isabel. I just want what is best for our shelter."

"I understand what you are trying to say, Sister Greenory." Isabel stood from behind her desk. "Trust me, I do."

54

# CHAPTER EIGHT

In Fred's mind, the white tent peaks lacing the edge of the clear blue sky looked like stiff dollops of meringue on a key-lime pie. *'Isabel Calhoun makes great key-lime pie.'* The hellish imp gripping tightly onto his brain stem plucked it like a banjo string to create a titillating chord at the thought.

And it was true. Isabel made key-lime pie for every bake sale and Christmas get-together. She said the secret was to keep it cold, and it always was. Like a soft spoonful of ice sitting on his hot tongue, sizzling like soft serve on asphalt until it washed down his throat.

Without air-conditioning in his car, just the *thought* of that cold key-lime pie was a godsend. He made a U-turn and drove past the tent twice while thinking about it. The third time, he actually stopped to look.

It was a big ol' tent, the kind he was used to seeing during a good old-fashioned revival. Of course, Jerry would never be caught dead stamping his feet in the Texas grass. The church building was all *modern-ized* now, so revival was always held inside. It didn't matter that the pews couldn't hold all the bodies that crammed themselves through the door when it came time to repent and renew their relationship with the Lord. If it was standing room only, that stroked Jerry's ego mighty well.

'*Puffy windbag.*' The imp's voice snorted and snarled.

Fred smiled and removed his cap to scratch at the back of his head. He couldn't disagree.

The white tent was double the size of any church building he had ever seen. He parked his car in the grass and his worn leather boots left impressions in the soft earth. Fred bit the gristle of his cheek and stuck his hands in his pockets as he walked around, ducking his head low in case anyone came tearing out looking for a fight.

Although from what he could tell, the tent was completely empty.

A naked, dead tree loomed close to its entrance. Its withered branches sagged with the unseen burden of its centuries. Each spidery twig bulged out of knots that grew like pustules along the peeling brown bark.

Fred's shoulder jerked and his head swung to the side. He hissed through his teeth and shoved his cap back down over his ragged scalp.

*'Deeaatthhh,'* the imp's claws dug into his brain stem and he could *feel* the warm juices drain down his spine.

Fred's shoulder jerked again. He ground his teeth so hard that they hurt.

"S-stop!" He swatted at the back of his head, dragging his nails dangerously close to where the staples began. The cap didn't cover everything, it was usually just enough to keep people from asking questions.

*'Death is here. Death is near.'*

"Stop!"

*'Death is going to munch your guts. Your bubbly, ugly, stinky guts.'*

Fred growled. He traipsed around the side of the tent, trying to get a glimpse underneath the edges. Nothing. He leaned in close until he was in danger of tripping over one of the wooden pegs.

Nothing.

*'Death tastes like rot. Worse than your brain.'*

"I can't wait to find a doctor who will yank you out with a pair of pliers," Frank snarled. "And I hope it hurts." He doubled back, going around the tent again from its rear and then walking up the opposite side. He did everything to avoid the entrance until that was the only thing left to peer through.

The front tent flap peeled back in front of his eyes, even though the material looked like it was heavy canvas and the breeze wasn't very strong. Fred swallowed hard and sniffed, scraping his hand across the tip of his itchy nose as he inched closer.

The tent flap waved at him until he caught the edge.

*'Don't want that.'* The imp rattled its claws against his skull. *'Don't want that, don't want that, don't want to go in there, stinky boy!'*

Fred swatted at the back of his head again and ducked inside.

His eyes took a moment to adjust to the sudden darkness. Inside it was like twilight, and the pinpricks of sunlight straining to squeeze through the holes in the canvas mimicked a thousand stars. Dust swirled around in twisters with a smell like it had come from his grandmother's attic. Fred stuck his hands back down into his pockets and fingered his keys, using the jagged metal teeth to keep himself grounded.

*'Tomb,'* the imp said.

"Shut *up*," Fred hawked and spat.

Rows and rows of white aluminum chairs lined either side of the narrow grass walkway like teeth, or tombstones, Fred couldn't decide which. After the very last row, there was a rough platform that seemed to be made of carpet stapled to some plywood. It wasn't very wide, but it was just enough to support the pulpit that rose proudly from its center.

The pulpit was stained bright red, and it smelled strongly of cedar. The cross on its face was burnished brass, polished to a shine to where he could see his reflection. Fred stood in front of the pulpit and looked back towards the rows of chairs.

'*Teeth,*' he thought conclusively.

The tent's sides rippled. The sudden flapping of canvas was enough to jerk Fred out of his reverie and send him flying back down the walkway. He didn't even know why he was running, just that he suddenly been taken over by a strong case of the *heebie jeebies.*

'*No good,*' the imp attached to his brain kept whispering over and over. '*No good. No good. No good.*'

For half a second, he didn't think he would make it.

Fred staggered out the entrance and then stumbled as he stepped in a gopher hole. He crashed to his knees and ripped his cap off his head, gripping the bill as he slammed it into the ground.

"Damn it! Damn it! Goddamn *fuck* it!"

Swearing didn't fix the pain that spiked through his knee, but it made him feel better.

He paused after his tirade to take a deep breath. Fred punched the center of his cap to knock out the dents and then placed it back on top of his head. He dragged it down towards his brow, growling out the last of his frustrations.

Just as he was recovering, a long shadow caught his attention.

Fred sprang to his feet so quickly that he almost tripped over the gopher hole twice. His breath barreled through his chest and got stuck in his perpetually stopped-up nose.

It looked like a man. But then, how long had someone been standing there, watching him? And it was unnaturally tall, even as far as shadows went. Fred pressed his hand against his chest, only suddenly aware of how fast his heart was beating.

*'Don't, don't, don't.'* The imp was twisting around in his skull so violently that Fred's head started spinning. *'Don't turn, don't turn, don't look, don't look-!'*

Then in a sudden, rapid movement, the shadow sprouted wings. A gust of wind brushed against the back of Fred's neck and he yelped, leaping over the gopher hole and spinning around, his hand going down to his empty hip.

His Colt was in the car. *God-fucking-damnit!*

He didn't know what he expected to see. A man, maybe. A man with wings? An angel?

But there wasn't anything like that. All he saw was a vulture, with its bald red head and hunched black shoulders, perched on a skeletal branch of the naked tree.

Fred let out a harsh laugh. "Stupid bird!" His rancor covered up his relief. He pounded his chest again, as if the force would slow its thumping. "God, stupid bird. If I had my pistol, you'd be dinner!"

He didn't even look at the tent again. Fred turned and started walking back towards his car, digging around in his pockets and fumbling with his keys while he muttered.

"Stupid bird. Stupid tent." His shoulder and head jerked at the same time. "Stupid, stupid!"

*'You're stupid,'* the imp sneered. Fred ignored it.

# CHAPTER NINE

The criminal temperature plummet inside the Super Value was downright polar. Faye had to keep her hands stuck inside the pockets of her jacket just to stop her fingers from going numb in-between customers.

There was very little traffic, even for a Monday. People had that post-church hangover, she supposed. It seemed to get worse every week.

One of her coworkers walked by and held up a pack of cigarettes. She nodded at him vaguely and hunched her shoulders forward in anticipation of the chill that would settle in after the rush of warmth. Her windbreaker rustled and the door swung open to usher in a gust of hot air, along with the faint smell of stale cigarette smoke that flowed from her coworker's knotted mop.

She sometimes envied his ability to take multiple ten-minute cigarette breaks throughout the day—far more than their allotted two. But she didn't envy that kind of money-sucking addiction. She had enough of those of her own, as evidenced by the twin half-empty glass bottles of Dr. Pepper that sat next to her register.

"You've got to love the smell of it." A voice she didn't know jerked her free from her thoughts. Faye whipped her head around and stared at the man standing across from her on the other side of the conveyor belt.

"Hey," she said automatically. "How's it going?" She reached for his purchase while still fully processing the image of the person in front of her.

He was *tall*. Absurdly tall. The top of his greying head looked ready to scrape the ceiling tiles. His skin was the same mottled, sickly color as the bass getting warm on ice shavings behind the glass deli counter. He dropped a pack of Newports into her hand, and she noticed that his thick nails were as white as milk.

He smiled at her with a mouth full of crooked teeth.

"$1.70," she said. Her voice cracked and she tried to cover it up by clearing her throat.

"There was a time when you could buy commercial cigarettes for five cents," the man said.

Faye tried not to roll her eyes.

"And there was a time when women didn't vote," she said. "$1.70?" She flexed her fingers, eager to ring him up and get him out of there.

The man looked towards the entrance as he rifled through his pockets. His bony fingers bulged obscenely against the fabric already wrapped tightly around his thighs.

"Quite a storm we're about to get," he said. He talked slow, like the people who lived out West in Gulper's Gorge where the town was so small that their entire police force was one sleepy sheriff and two deputies. Slow, like he had all the time in the world, and like the Super Value didn't close at 7PM.

"Sure," Faye said. "Might wanna get home before it starts." She was well-aware of the angry grey clouds gathering on the horizon. She wasn't looking forward to the rain that would make her air-conditioned hell feel even colder.

"This town will be glad for the rain." He turned his gaze towards her, a deep-set pair of lavender eyes so pale that their edges faded in with the whites.

And yet, they were the youngest part about him.

Faye's stomach started doing splits. "It can get really dry around here," she agreed. That was about all she could manage. She still had one hand out, waiting for his payment, and her fingertips were starting to go numb.

She wished, at the very least, that her coworker would come back inside and break the spell.

Instead of responding immediately, the man picked up the package of Newports from the belt. He broke it open and slid out a white cigarette, holding it out to her like he was offering a sacrament.

Faye completely froze.

"I don't smoke," she said quietly.

"Would you say that tobacco is the vice of choice for Sweet Providence?" the man asked. "It's all right. I'm just a preacher with a wondering."

"Maybe," she said. She looked back towards the glass doors. All she could see of her coworker was the back of his head. "Tobacco is a big one. Whiskey and beer is another. I mean...isn't that the case everywhere?"

"Not necessarily," the man said. He held up the cigarette a little higher. "Do you enjoy the taste of whiskey, or beer?"

"Not really," she told him. She pressed her hand against her stomach to try and quell the dangerous churning. If it turned anymore, she was going to have to make a run for the bathroom. "I don't much care for the taste."

He drew the cigarette away and placed it between his own shriveled lips. The man pulled a white card from the breast pocket of his blazer and offered that instead.

"You've seen that big tent out on Deer Head?" he asked.

Faye nodded.

"We're having a revival service there on Wednesday night," he said. "The Lord wants you there."

This time, Fay couldn't stop the aggravated expression from spreading across her face.

"Thanks," she said. "I already have a church."

"It's not a church I'm trying to offer you," he said. "It's an answer."

Another second snuck past, then Faye took the card. She told herself that it was just to appease the man and get him to leave. And at the very least, he seemed satisfied. The man tucked the pack of Newports into his pocket and placed a wide-brimmed black hat on top of his head.

"*We gather together*," he started singing, *"To sing His pr-ai-ses. O-h H-oly, Oh H-oly Jesus…"* he walked away. Only when he was gone did Faye realize she never finished ringing him up.

She closed out the purchase, even though it would make the drawer short, and then propped the white card against one of her Dr. Pepper bottles. The name on the front looked hand-typed, black ink letters marching across the surface like a line of army ants.

REV. APOSTLE GRIEVANCE.

# CHAPTER TEN

ews about the big white tent on Deer Head Road was springing off every tongue within hours of the first sighting. By late Wednesday afternoon, cars filled with curious heads were creeping along the dirt path, trying to be as inconspicuous as possible as they found somewhere to park within the nearby grass. Visitors edged in with uncertainty, no one wanting to be the singular fool who ventured onto private property if there was nothing going on.

From somewhere behind the folds, the tinny chords of a keyboard struck up a lively gospel tune. It lifted the burdens off a few faces and caused a few exchanged glances before feet began to shuffle forward with new confidence. Two-by-two, the assembled bodies all poured in through the wide entrance.

Among their number were Faye Warren and Ezra Buchanan. On a normal Wednesday night, Ezra would have been at Jerry's church, but he couldn't say 'no' to Faye. Even though he had no interest in some traveling preacher's hokey revival gimmick. All she had to do was give him one long look with those round, pitiful eyes and he was jelly.

Right off the bat, though, he didn't like the smell of the place. There was nothing homey about a big white canvas staked down in the middle of a dying, brown field. As they ducked through the entrance, he was immediately hit with all the familiar smells of Old Spice cologne and carpet shampoo, even though the only carpeting was the dingy scrap stapled to a ramshackle platform at the very end of the rows. Whoever had arranged the metal folding chairs had also made sure to leave a very clear, narrow aisle down the center. Ezra shuffled down as far as possible to look for an empty seat that wouldn't leave him with his crutch awkwardly shoved between him and a stranger.

"I thought there would be more people," Faye admitted. She claimed a seat at the far-end of the second row and Ezra took the chair next to her.

"It looks like a good crowd to me," Ezra said. "It's just a roomy space." Now that he was settled, he could focus on the churning in his guts.

"Sorry if this is a dud," Faye muttered. "I don't know why I thought this was a good idea."

"Something different?" Ezra offered with a small smile. "Something not-Jerry?"

"Yeah," she said. "Maybe that's it."

The gospel hymn notes started to wind down. Ezra finally pulled his eyes away from the gathering crowd and shifted his focus towards the pulpit. The keyboard was also sitting on the carpeted plywood, and the man bent over its keys was either way too tall for his seat, or it was a much smaller instrument than Ezra assumed. The man's knees were bunched up underneath the keyboard so that it looked like it was sitting in his lap, even though it was nestled properly on a tall steel stand. His shoulders were hunched up almost to his ears and his neck was stooped like a crane's while his long, spindly fingers crawled across the brown-and-ivory plastic. When the man finally looked up, he stopped playing, and the silence was unbearably heavy.

"Jesus," Ezra muttered under his breath. "Check out the crypt keeper over there."

"That's the man who came into my store," Faye whispered back. "I told you he was tall."

"You didn't mention that he was also a thousand."

"It didn't feel as important."

The man, who Ezra assumed to be the reverend, moved away from the keyboard and went to stand behind the red pulpit. He made it look like a child's toy, with the bent microphone pointing towards the very middle of his ribs.

"What a glorious evening to be gathered here today, in the presence of God Almighty," the reverend spoke. His resonant voice was much stronger than Faye had described it, with a dark timbre and only a slight hint of a rasp underneath it. His teeth were all brown, and they made his lurid purple lips look ghastly. Even though he wore a nice suit and his lavender silk tie matched his eyes, if Ezra met him on the street, he wouldn't hand him two cents.

"Amen," popcorned through the crowd. Ezra's mouth was too dry to say anything.

"Amen," Faye whispered. For some reason, it was *her* response that made his pulse quicken and the hair on the back of his neck stand up.

"Now, I know that for many of you, I am not your usual pastor," the reverend continued. "And I thank you all for coming here today and giving me a chance. It has been many years since I have been in Sweet Providence—" he rested a hand against his chest, "and it bereaves me to say that not very much has changed at all." He brought his hand down and slammed it on top of the pulpit. Ezra jumped in his seat.

"'But what do you mean by that, Reverend Grievance?' you might ask me. And I will say to you, that Sweet Providence is a town steeped in sin. I see you shaking your head, there." He pointed condemningly towards the crowd, singling out a tall man in the fourth row. "I will ask you this; do you think that the people of Sodom and Gomorrah knew their own wickedness before God sent fire from the sky to destroy them? But here," he held up both hands, "how many of you love a nice, cold glass of sweet tea in the summertime? You, you—and I can certainly say that I do. I know that all of us do. But how is sweet tea made? You take pure, cold water—water without a blemish—and you *dump* in the tea bags, you *pour* in the sugar, and that water gets real dirty. And what do you do? You have to let it steep. Then the water isn't water anymore, but it sure does taste sweet, and we love it, don't we? Well, think of Sweet Providence as a pitcher of water. Then the devil walks over and he drops in a tea bag. He says, 'don't worry, you'll like how it tastes!' And he drops in another, and another. The devil likes his tea strong, after all, and tea is bitter, just like sin. So he has to dump that sugar in there and stir it up—and once he gets you all good and stirred up, that is what he serves you. You think there's nothing wrong with it, because it tastes so good! Sin is supposed to feel a little good, isn't it? But what happens if that's all you drink?"

Ezra rubbed his face. He was already trying his hardest to stay awake, and he was losing the battle.

"Without any water, your kidneys will start making stones. And God doesn't want you walking around with all those stones dragging you down. He wants to give you good, pure water." Grievance's eye swept over the crowd again. "You." He pointed to the other side of the room. Ezra couldn't see far enough to pick out a distinct face at the end of that finger. "What is your name?"

There was rustling as more heads turned.

"Betty," a woman's voice responded, sounding nervous or at the very least, displeased at having been singled out.

"Come up here, Sister Betty," the reverend stepped around his pulpit. Bodies shuffled around and Ezra watched as a woman the same age as his mother with short silver hair walked up towards the platform.

"Tell me, Sister," the reverend took the woman's hands in his own, "what ails you?"

Betty stared up at his face like he was reading her mind. "The doctors told me that I have a detached retina in my right eye, and I'm half-blind in the other," she said. "I can't see very well."

"A detached retina sounds mighty painful, sister. And now I have to ask you, what color are my eyes?"

Grievance asked. The woman furrowed her brow and shook her head.

"I don't rightly know," she said, her voice quivering. "I can't focus that well."

Grievance let go of one of her hands so he could set his palm against her forehead. His long fingers bent and gripped her scalp. "What have the doctors said that you need to do?" Grievance raised his voice, and Ezra flinched.

"I need surgery," Betty's voice broke. "They need to take out my eye and fix the problem before the put it back in."

"The doctors want to take out this woman's eye!" Grievance announced. "But by the mighty grace and goodness of God, she will be healed, and her sight will be restored!" His other hand grasped her shoulder, and he held her so tightly that she trembled visibly in his hold. "In the name of the Father, and the Son, and the Holy Spirit—by the might of our God, who sits on high amongst the saints and the angels—*you will be healed!*"

The woman let out a sharp cry. Faye dissolved into tears. She rocked forward and hunched over her lap, burying her face in her hands. Ezra set his hand on her back, momentarily too distracted to even care about Betty.

"Faye," he whispered. "Faye? Are you okay?"

"Oh, my God!" the woman cried out. "Thank God! I can see!"

"Sister!" The reverend's voice kept rising. "What color are my eyes?"

"Purple, reverend! Purple like the robes of Jesus!"

Faye started crying even harder. Ezra wrapped both arms around her and pulled her close, rocking gently back and forth to try and soothe her.

"Faye, Faye, what's the matter?" he asked softly.

In the rows behind them, metal clanged as people jumped from their seats. Everyone in attendance was shouting and praising God, except for Ezra—all he wanted to do was shrink into the ground and take Faye with him. It was so loud that the sound alone made his heart feel like it was going to jump out of his chest.

"I need to be healed," Faye sobbed. "I am sick, I am a sinner—I need to be healed—"

"What are you talking about?" Ezra stroked her hair. "You're not a sinner, Faye—you're not sick. You're young. You're healthy." He turned his head back towards the pulpit, and a long shadow fell over Faye's bent form.

The reverend was standing in front of them, with only a metal chair to separate him from Faye.

"Is something wrong?" the reverend asked. His voice was close enough not to be drowned out by the wailing and singing behind him.

"Reverend." Faye let out a strangled gasp. "I am so sick!" She uncurled and her body tensed like she was going to throw herself at him. Ezra kept his arm in front of her as a barrier, but the reverend reached out instead. Grievance set his hands on either side of Faye's flushed face, his long thumbs wiping away the streams of tears that flowed from her pretty eyes.

"No, Ms. Warren," he said. "It is not sickness inside of you, it is God. He seeks to save countless souls and bathe them in the blood of His Son through you. Are you willing to let him?"

"Yes!" Faye choked. "Yes, yes, I want to be used...I want to be used by God!"

Grievance pulled Faye's head forward and pressed his lips against her crown, pulling her out of Ezra's arms completely.

Ezra's blood suddenly felt like ice in his veins. He didn't know what to say, so he just watched Faye cling to the reverend's arms and soak his dark sleeves with her tears.

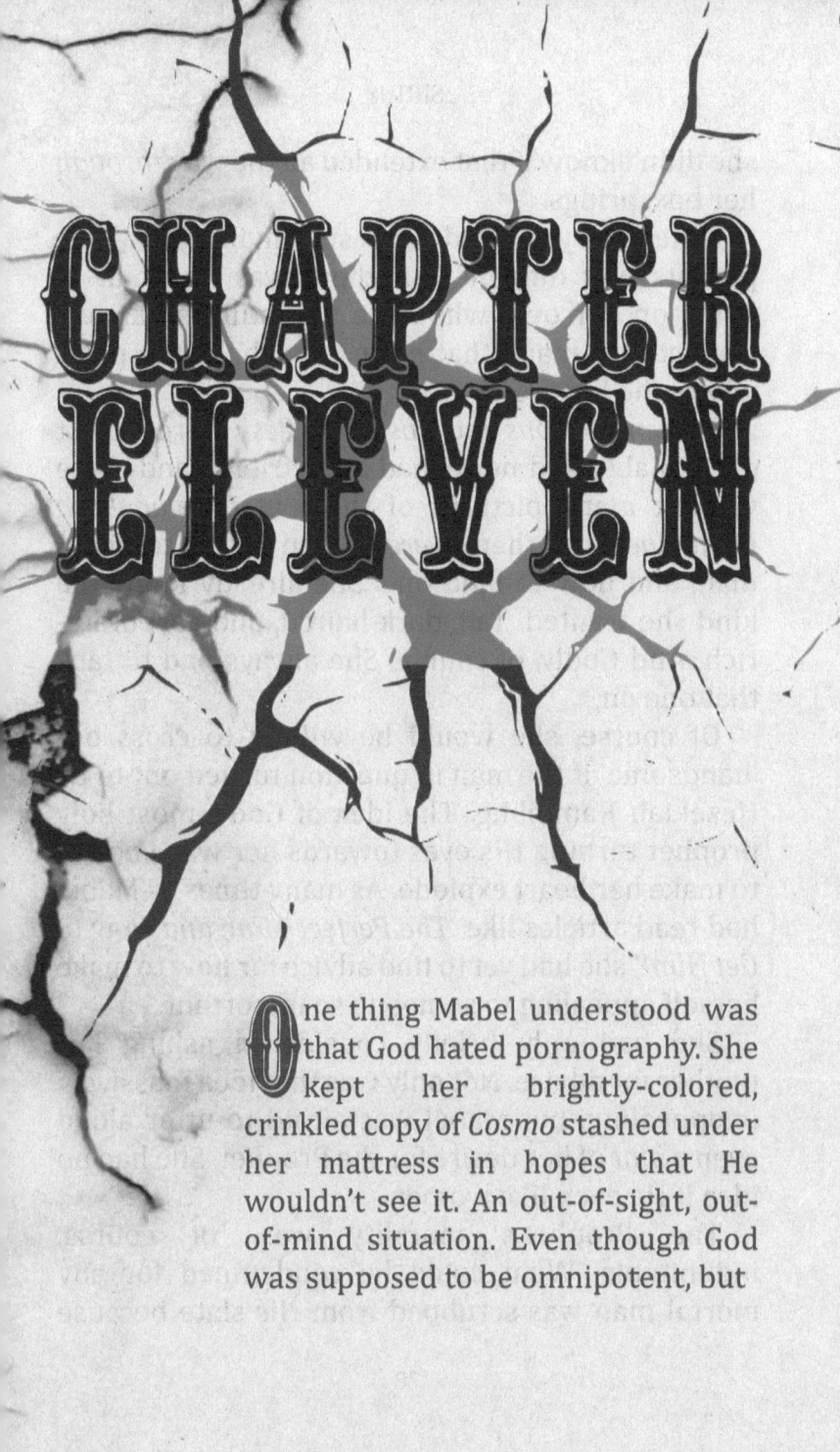

# CHAPTER ELEVEN

One thing Mabel understood was that God hated pornography. She kept her brightly-colored, crinkled copy of *Cosmo* stashed under her mattress in hopes that He wouldn't see it. An out-of-sight, out-of-mind situation. Even though God was supposed to be omnipotent, but she didn't know if that extended all the way *through* her boxsprings.

Nineteen years-old and still living with her parents was difficult, but there was no point in living on her own while she was still unmarried. Her mother made that clear enough, to the point where the lectures
about *temptations* and *sins of the flesh* were almost daily. Mabel had never had a boyfriend, and there weren't many pictures of them in *Cosmopolitan Magazine*—but there *were* tips on where to find a man, and how to land one. She already knew the kind she wanted. Tall, dark-haired, and corporate-rich. And Godly, of course. She always had to tack that one on.

Of course, she would be willing to cross out 'handsome' if the man in question turned out to be Hezekiah Ramplling. The idea of God's most holy prophet turning His eyes towards her was enough to make her heart explode. As many times as Mabel had read articles like *'The Perfect Man, and How to Get Him!',* she had yet to find advice for how to make herself appealing to someone so important.

She had only briefly considered asking her mother for advice. Not only was that idea massively unappealing, but Mabel was afraid to utter aloud even a *hint* of her desire for the Prophet. She had no idea if He even like women.

The Prophet's morality was, of course, indubitable. What could be condemned for any mortal man was scrubbed from His slate because

He carried the very words from God's mouth in His own.

Mabel rolled over onto her back and set her magazine on top of her face. She felt bad for even fostering the doubt, but she couldn't help but wonder if she could change Him.

There were no articles in *Cosmo* entitled, *'The Perfect Man, and How to Straighten Him Out!'*

A knock on the front door pulled her out of her self-pity spiral. Mabel jumped and rolled up her magazine, launching herself over the side of her bed to stuff it under her mattress. The knock came again, and she staggered off the side of the bed, hopping on one foot to shake out the pins-and-needles out of the other.

Mabel's bedroom door opened up into the living room, which was then only a few feet from the front door. Her parents put her there deliberately, so that there was no chance of anything being snuck under their nose.

Mabel was finally able to set both feet on the floor and take a look through the peephole.

Prophet Hezekiah stood on the front porch, His pale face made golden by the yellow porch light. Behind Him, another man with curly red hair stood by a crummy station wagon that was mostly cast in shadow. Mabel knew the redhead's name, but she could never remember it.

Her fingers trembled and slipped over the door's brass hardware as she tried to unlock everything at breakneck speed. She pulled the door open, and the fresh night air sucked all the breath out of her. Belatedly, she remembered that she was in her pajamas.

"Good evening," the Prophet spoke. His corrupted eye rolled in one direction while His good baby-blue kept its focus on her. Mabel forgot every word in the English language that she ever knew. Her knees felt weak as jelly underneath her nightgown.

"Good evening," she finally managed to say. She looked past the Prophet's shoulder to see if the redhead was going to join Him, but then quickly pulled back her focus. "Is everything all right?"

"Where are your parents?" Hezekiah asked. He stepped inside without being invited and shut the door behind Him. Clearly, the redhead would not be joining.

"My mother is still at the church." Mabel's voice faltered as she took half a step back. "My father is asleep."

"Thank you," the Prophet said. He did not elaborate further, nor did He apologize for showing up unannounced. He walked right past Mabel, headed for her father's bedroom. She skittered back a few more steps and watched Him move, torn between running back to her own room and trying to interfere.

Her father would certainly have something to say if she let the Prophet wake him up. Then again, she had already been perceived far more than she cared to be while wearing a pink flowery nightgown.

In the end, she decided that her father could handle himself. She ran back to her bedroom and shut the door.

# CHAPTER TWELVE

Jerry's headboard creaked and he spread his legs a little wider, trying to stay relaxed as he backed himself down onto the thick dildo that was suction cupped to the wood. The soft, squelching sounds of lube and his own, sweaty skin were driving him wild—and he could only hope that his TV was loud enough to

drown it all out. Jerry lowered his head and dug his hands into his mattress, taking a deep breath to try and swallow a loud groan as he finally pushed himself all the way down to the base. He allowed himself a moment of reprieve, grinding
down onto the dildo while the headboard cracked dangerously before he rocked his hips forward and slid back up the hard silicone.

His bedroom door swung open, and Jerry yelled. He froze, still half-penetrated and gripping his white cotton sheets.

Hezekiah was good enough to close the door, and He did not even flick on the light. The Prophet walked over until He was standing next to the TV, His scarecrow-figure briefly illuminated by the eerie blue light.

"Don't stop on my account," the Prophet said dryly.

"Jesus Christ, Zeke!" Jerry gasped. He resumed his slide, determined to pull off the dildo without ripping his anus open. "Don't you know how to knock? And who the hell let you in?" He froze again. "Isabel-?"

"She is still at the church, I've been told." Hezekiah chose a spot close to the edge of the bed and sat down. "Your daughter was good enough to open the door." The Prophet gripped the bottom of the dildo and broke its suction. Jerry couldn't stop himself from groaning as it moved, and then choked on a gasp when Hezekiah thrust it back inside.

"Shit!" The pastor clawed at his sheets. "Be careful with that!"

"Do you want me to stop?" The Prophet asked coolly.

"No," Jerry panted. "But it's not a damn butter churn."

Hezekiah sucked on His teeth loudly, apparently unimpressed, but was a lot gentler the second time as He worked the dildo back and forth, twisting it around so that Jerry felt every inflated vein.

"It has happened," Hezekiah said. The inflection in His voice never changed. "Just as I told you that it would."

"What has?" Jerry asked. He raised his head to focus on the TV screen, not wanting to keep his face buried while being handled. That was a little *too* intimate.

"The Dark Reverend has come." Hezekiah picked up the pace. "Tonight marks the beginning of the End of Days."

"How do you figure *that?*" Jerry moaned.

Hezekiah twisted the dildo a full rotation and then slammed it all the way inside. Jerry felt the tickle of the tip all the way up in his throat and he coughed. His tight ring of muscle spasmed around the thick base, clenching and unclenching with no reprieve. Hezekiah kept His palm flat against the base and His fingers clenched Jerry's ass, holding the damn thing in like He was plugging a leak in a fishing boat.

"You do not like to heed me," Hezekiah said. "But you can no longer ignore the words of God. In the coming days, there will be sickness and pain such as we have not seen in a hundred years. You *must* mark me on it, Jerry Calhoun. The earth will open up and it will swallow every single soul who ever turned their face from God."

"And what comes after that?" Jerry sounded a little strangled. He coughed again. "What is the light at the end of this tunnel? I can't just deliver a message like that to the congregation without giving them something to hope for.

"Their hope?" Hezekiah's fingers dug into Jerry's flesh until the pastor could no longer feel his left cheek. "Their hope is for a quick death, and for the mercy of St. Peter."

"Not good enough—" Jerry began. His words were cut off by a sharp gasp that came tearing out past his teeth as Hezekiah ripped out the dildo. The prophet dropped it in the middle of his back, and the heavy thump cleared his sinuses. Jerry couldn't wait to see *that* bruise.

"The Dark Reverend held his first service tonight," Hezekiah said. "What were *you* doing, Jerry? Giving some anecdote about potato salad?"

Jerry set his teeth and dropped onto his side. Everything from his ribs to his ankles ached like he had been beaten. He gave himself a second and then propped himself up on his elbow before craning his head to look at the prophet. "I know you don't like my style of preaching, but it keeps them faithful and in their seats."

"It won't be enough," Hezekiah warned. "They don't want to feel good and mollified anymore. They want to feel the *fire*. They want to see their faith made flesh. They will find it somewhere else, if they can't get it from you."

"So, you want me to start shaking them up a little bit? Challenging them? I can do that," Jerry said. "But I can't have you following me around, talking doomsday and getting everybody's dander up. I know, I know," he held up his hand. "You're the Prophet of God. But that doesn't mean he didn't scramble your brains when he hit you with that lightning bolt. Twice."

Hezekiah's mouth quirked. The Prophet Chariot did not smile often, but when He did, it made Jerry nauseous.

"Scrambled," Hezekiah mused aloud. "Like the Tower of Babel. You and I are speaking different languages now."

"But we have the same goal," Jerry urged back. "We both want to see souls saved."

"Is that what you've been reaching for?" Hezekiah asked. "I wouldn't have guessed." He stood up, sliding his one good eye up and down Jerry's body like a hunter examining a deer carcass for cleaning. "I'll let myself out. I'm sure Mrs. Izzy will be back soon."

"God." Jerry had forgotten about his wife. The underside of his balls itched so furiously that he wanted to rip them off, but he drew the line at scratching himself in front of God's Chosen Prophet. "Who drove you here? I can take you home."

"Jonah. And there is no need." Hezekiah motioned dismissively. "He is waiting just outside."

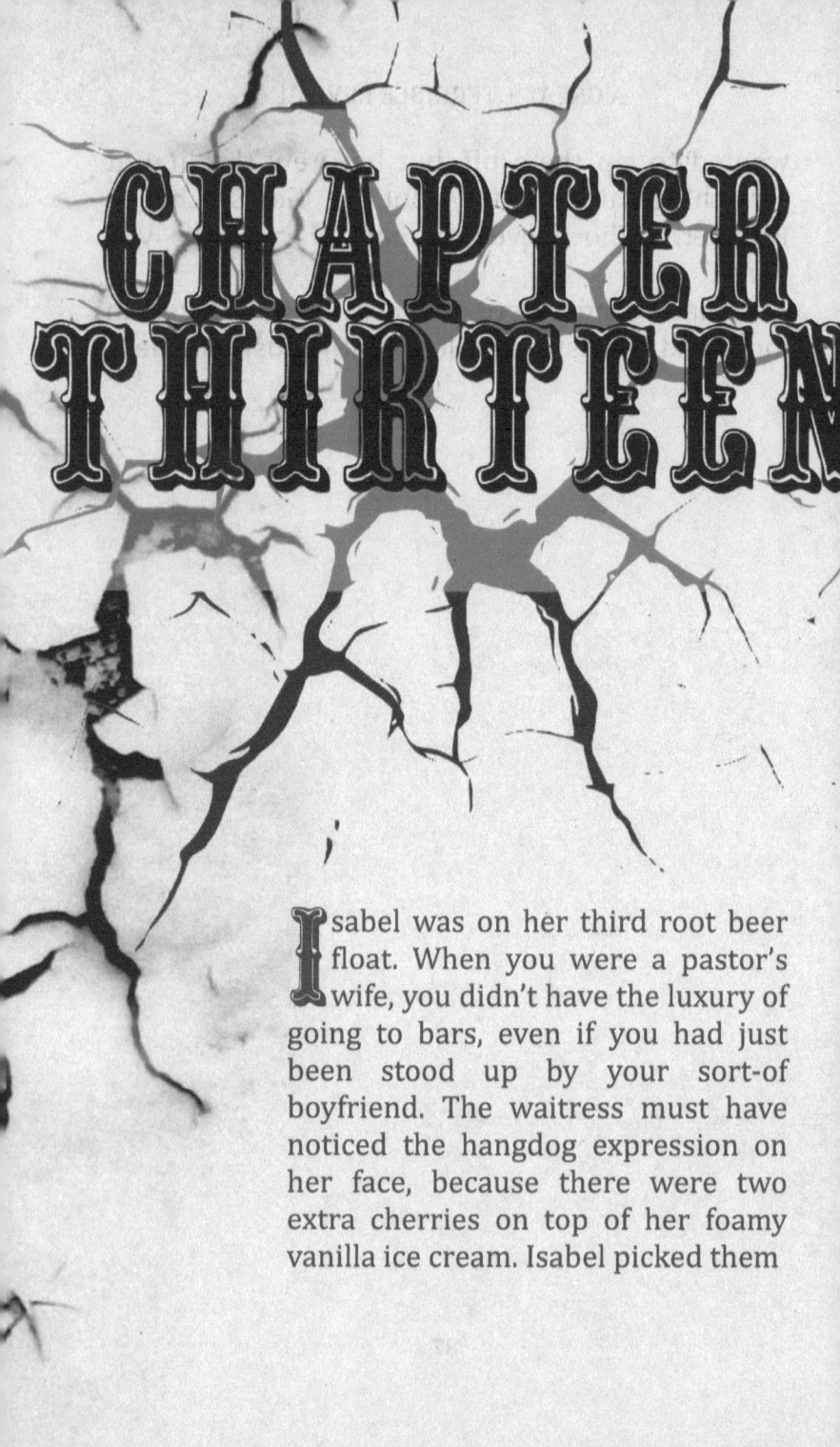

# CHAPTER THIRTEEN

Isabel was on her third root beer float. When you were a pastor's wife, you didn't have the luxury of going to bars, even if you had just been stood up by your sort-of boyfriend. The waitress must have noticed the hangdog expression on her face, because there were two extra cherries on top of her foamy vanilla ice cream. Isabel picked them off, one by one, and sucked off the plump red fruit before chewing on the hard end of the stem. She set the shredded bits down on her napkin and then folded them out of sight. By the time she was finished with the cherries, her ice cream had settled nicely into her soda, and all it needed was a good stir.

The smell of peppermint mixed with leather and cologne caught her nose. Isabel pressed her lips together and purposefully did not look up. Even so, she caught a glimpse of Jonah's red hair as he slid into the booth right across from her.

"I'm sorry," he said before anything else.

"For what?" She finally looked up. "How did you know I would be here?"

"You always come here when you're sad," he answered. "And I..." A smile sprang to his face and he cut himself off, turning to greet the waitress who had migrated their way with a pink pad of paper ready in her hand. "Nothing for me, thank you—actually, do you have any lemon pie?"

"Sure do," the waitress said, smiling back. There was a little extra glimmer in her eye when she spoke to him. Isabel couldn't blame her for it. Jonah had that effect.

"Great," Jonah said. "I'll take a slice of that, then, and some Coke, please."

"You've got it." The waitress turned back to Isabel. "Are you still good over here, darlin'? Or can I get you anything else?"

"I am fine," Isabel said. "Thank you."

The waitress walked away, and Jonah turned his attention back to Isabel.

"I *am* sorry," he said. "I was with—I had to drive." His eyes pleaded with Isabel to understand. And she did. Even though he did not dare speak Hezekiah's name aloud, she knew exactly what he was trying to tell her.

She didn't blame him, but she didn't like it, either.

"I'm not angry," she said. "I'm just tired." She stirred her root beer float with her straw. "The service ran late, and then I had to count up the offering and close everything up."

"Why did Jerry leave so early?" He lowered his voice when speaking about her husband, but not out of reverence or fear like he did for Hezekiah. It was more like he couldn't stand to have the taste of Jerry's name in his mouth. Isabel pursed her lips.

"He took Mabel home," she said. "He never sticks around for long on Wednesday nights."

"Sounds like you do a lot more work than he does," Jonah scoffed. Isabel shrugged.

Their conversation suffered another pause as the waitress returned and set Jonah's lemon pie and a glass of Coke in front of him. He thanked her sweetly and dug in before she even walked off.

The flush in the waitress' cheeks *did* irritate Isabel, just a little. And she didn't necessarily care that it was hypocritical to feel that way.

"It's just the way things are," Isabel resumed. "Pastors' wives all over the country lament their wageless positions. I'm sure the same can be said for prophets' sluts." She didn't really mean to let loose the last word, but it came flying out before she could stop it. Isabel sucked on her teeth but held Jonah's gaze, wondering if he could see her flinch.

Jonah stopped chewing the bite of lemon pie that was in his mouth. He stared at her for a long minute and then swallowed, glancing down to stab at a rogue piece of crust on his plate.

"Charity work doesn't pay too well," he said with a tight smile. This time, Isabel could not stop herself from rolling her eyes.

"Come on, Jonah." She leaned forward far enough that her elbows twinged from being pressed so hard against the table. "It isn't charity work for you. There's something that you get out of it. What is it, besides the food you eat and the bed where you sleep? There's influence in it too, right?"

Jonah's eye twitched. "I like it better when you talk pretty," he said. "This is not what I come here for."

"Well, you brought up Jerry first," she pointed out. "And I know why *I* stay. Forget the fact that he would make my life a living Hell. I count the money. I know where it goes. I *like* knowing where it is and how much he has, how much goes towards Mabel's college, and how much gets allocated to the Cabinet and the soup kitchen and to the deacons."

"How much gets allocated to *you*?" Jonah challenged.

"Wageless, like I said." Isabel sipped her float.

"Sure." Jonah sat back. "But you don't go without. You make sure of that. And I think that's the biggest difference."

"How do you figure?" Isabel asked.

"You have a nice car. Your hair is always done. You *look* the part. A well-kept wife is a sign of a successful pastor. A shabby partner is the sign of a successful prophet."

Isabel shook her head. "Two different interpretations of the Gospels, I reckon," she said. "God knows that those two have plenty differences to clash over."

"I know," Jonah said. He stared at her as he spoke. He had abandoned his lemon pie, and his glass was drained dry with the exception of a very slowly melting pile of ice cubes. He crossed his arms over his chest and tucked his hands into his armpits like he was hugging himself.

Isabel didn't want what was left of her root beer, either.

"I should get going," Isabel finally said. "It's late."

"I should settle up too," Jonah agreed. "I'll walk you to your car."

They paid their tabs separately with Jonah waiting behind her in line. She barely glanced up when it was his turn, waiting near the register while digging through her purse for her car key.

He held the door open for her and together, they walked around the side of the building, never once touching. They made small talk as they got further away from her car, and the shadows took over the parking lot.

Jonah used his hand to cushion her bare ass as he pinned her up against the brick wall. Isabel felt like that was very considerate of him.

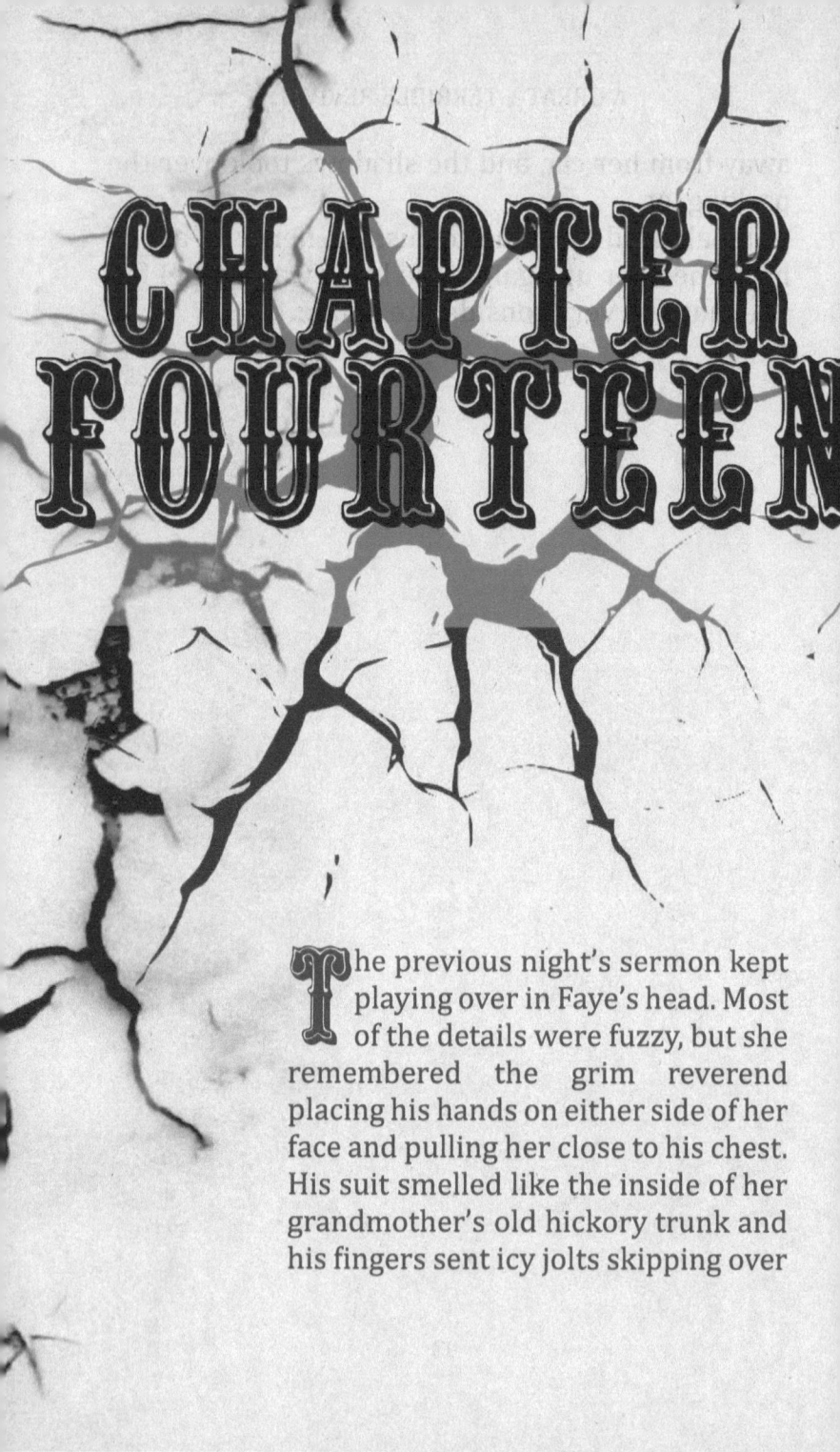

# CHAPTER FOURTEEN

The previous night's sermon kept playing over in Faye's head. Most of the details were fuzzy, but she remembered the grim reverend placing his hands on either side of her face and pulling her close to his chest. His suit smelled like the inside of her grandmother's old hickory trunk and his fingers sent icy jolts skipping over her red-hot cheeks. Faye couldn't even remember the last time someone had held her like that.

Faye adjusted the dial on her pricing gun and glanced up at the clock hanging just above the register.

Her coworker stood underneath, leaning against the belt and looking miserable. He had a nasty cough that sounded like a barking dog, but he hadn't been able to wheedle management into letting him knock off early.

"No matter how you look at it," he said miserably, "it's still two more hours to go until seven."

"I know." Faye looked down. She fiddled with the dial again and punched out a green tester sticker onto her hand. "You sound awful, Chris."

"I *feel* awful," Chris groaned. "I just need these next couple of hours to go by so I can go home and pass out." His words ended in another dry cough, and he grimaced. "I need a cigarette."

"Somehow, I think that is just going to make things worse." Faye grabbed a freezing block of vacuum-sealed chitterlings and slapped a green sticker onto the label. She hated unpackaging chitterlings the most. Even cold and wrapped in plastic, they still smelled like rotting guts.

"Can you cover for me?" Chris hacked and placed a hand against his bright red forehead. "I'll be fast."

Faye slapped down another row of green stickers and then abandoned the pricing gun and her cart. "Go fast," she said. "I still don't think it's going to help."

Chris broke away from the register before she could even finish talking. Within seconds he was out the door, his lighter already in his hand. She watched him lean against the window and let out that first puff of smoke.

The smoke swirled in the air, pulling his breath out on a line like a fishing wire.

The door alarm dinged, and a waft of tobacco slunk in behind Fred Presley as he walked in. He had his hands buried in the pockets of a dirty yellow-and-black letterman jacket and his head jerked towards his shoulder as soon as he walked through the door. Faye couldn't stop herself from pulling a face, so she looked away.

God knew, she *hated* Fred. There was nothing good about him, even before his accident. It used to be that she had to turn him away for trying to buy tall boys of piss-colored beer when he was already stinking intoxicated. Now, she had to stop him from trying to minister to her, even though they went to the same church.

He called her 'ladyboy', too, and she hated that. It made her want to punch him in the nose every time he let that particular slur fly.

"Lovely evening, Fay Wray." Fred circled around the registers and ended up in front of the stocked candy, picking over the colorfully wrapped chocolate bars.

"Wish I could see it," Faye told him. It wasn't really worth it, playing nice with Fred. She would do what she had to in order to keep her job, but she didn't really want to give him any ideas. And Fred could read 'take me' in a single word.

"Only two more hours." Fred picked up a Big Hunk bar and grinned. "Well, one hour and forty-five minutes." He jerked his head again and grimaced, flinging the candy bar back towards its box.

Faye took a deep breath to try and stop herself from smacking him away like a fly. "Yeah," she said. "Can't wait. Ezra's making pot roast."

She dropped Ezra's name whenever she could around Fred. He had no reason to know that they weren't still together.

"But there's revival tonight." Fred frowned. He picked up a 5th Avenue and gripped the crimped end, swinging it back and forth like a pendulum.

Faye raised her eyebrows and set her hand against her chest, feeling her heart skip a beat at the mention of revival, although she wasn't sure why. "Were you there last night?" she asked.

Fred smiled without showing any teeth. "Mhmm," he said. "Saw you and *Ezzzzra*," he dragged out the Z's as they buzzed off his tongue. "You was cryin' the whole time."

"No, I wasn't!" Faye spat. Fred grinned this time and snorted a laugh.

"Last night in the revival tent, Fay Wray turned in an Oscar-worthy performance!" He held up the candy bar like it was a microphone. "Never seen a face like that cry so pretty!"

"You're one to talk about faces, Fred Presley." Faye lowered her voice. She never liked to let it drop, but she would do it on purpose just to make men like him cringe. "Yours looks like it got hit by a tractor-trailer on its way to an ugly convention."

Fred's crooked top lip came up in a half-snarl. "I was *tryin'* to give you a compliment, *ladyboy*," he said. "It's hard to look pretty when you cry. There's snot and tears and peoples' chins get all wrinkled up. Not yours, though. Yours' got dimples."

A full-scale shudder of revulsion rippled from Faye's stomach to her throat and she felt like she was going to throw up. "Pick your candy, Fred."

Fred set the 5th Avenue bar on the conveyer belt. It was warm and melted in the middle from where he had been squeezing it. He grabbed the Big Hunk again and turned it around so that Faye could see the bold letters across the dark packaging.

"BIG HUNK!" Fred laughed like it was the funniest thing he had ever heard. He tossed the candy bar at Faye and then pulled a wad of damp, crumpled ones from his shirt pocket. "Will I see you at revival, Fay Wray?"

"That's not my name," Faye said. She punched the numbers in on the cash register so quickly that she almost chipped a nail.

*"Fay Wray, come play, come take me a-way,"* Fred sang each word as he dropped his crushed bills onto the conveyer belt. *"Take me to Hea-ven, I'll let you spin on my—"*

"Good*bye,* Fred!" Faye snarled. She grabbed his candy bars and threw them. "No one needs church here more than you!"

Fred caught the candy bars in his arms and grinned. He looked like he was about to say something else, but his expression completely evaporated when the front door came open and Chris walked back in, hacking up a lung.

"I'm going to die in this place, Faye," Chris wheezed.

"Cigarettes is bad for you, Chris West." Fred wagged his finger.

"I don't give a shit, Presley, lick my balls." Chris flashed Fred a different finger and hobbled towards the counter.

"Balls..." Fred frowned. "Chris West has *balls,* Fay Wray has..." he sucked his teeth. "*Pocket Billiards.*"

Faye couldn't stop herself, now that was Chris was back—there was nothing tying her to the register. She grabbed the sides of the conveyer belt and jumped, clearing the belt and knocking Fred in the shoulder with the heel of her combat boot. Fred howled and went down, flailing on his back like a beetle before rolling over onto his side.

"Jesus, Faye-!" Chris couldn't finish his sentence. He smothered a hard cough with his elbow, grabbing onto the belt so that his own wind didn't knock him over.

"I'm going to send you home to Heaven early, Fred, if you don't get out of my damn store!" Faye snarled. The rage that squeezed her chest was terrifying, but she liked the way it made her blood rush. Even though her head was spinning, she had full confidence in her ability to whoop Fred Presley's ass.

Fred scrambled to his feet and shoved his broken candy bars into his pockets. Blood trickled from his nose and into his mouth. He licked at it with his gross tongue.

"Sounds like you need the lord, sounds like you need *re-pent-in*," Fred smacked his lips. "Come on back down to revival, Fay."

Chris pulled his face out of his elbow and looked up. His skin was almost purple and his eyes looked bloodshot, like they were getting ready to pop out of his head.

Faye shot him a concerned look and shook her head. "Go on and get out, Fred. I've got bigger problems than you."

"BIGGER BALLS, TOO!" Fred shouted. Faye swung around, arm half-cocked, but Fred ducked and ran out the market door—cackling.

# CHAPTER FIFTEEN

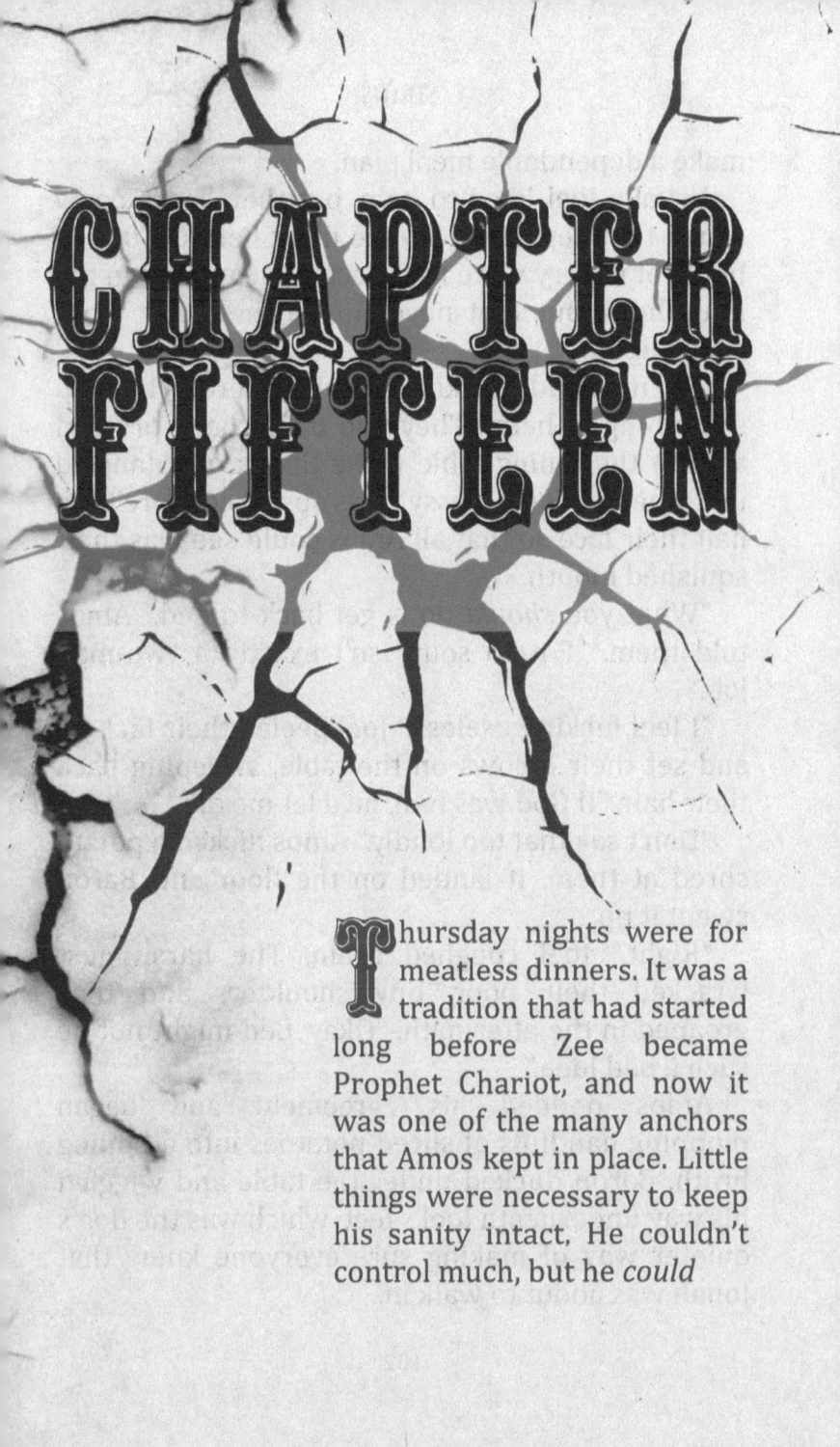

Thursday nights were for meatless dinners. It was a tradition that had started long before Zee became Prophet Chariot, and now it was one of the many anchors that Amos kept in place. Little things were necessary to keep his sanity intact. He couldn't control much, but he *could*

make a dependable meal plan.

Usually Joel liked to help, but they had a nasty cough that kept them up the night before. Sudden bouts of misery were not exactly uncommon in the household, but that never made them any more convenient.

"I'm not dead, you know," Joel muttered. "I can do something to help." They had their cheek pressed against the dining table while their arms dangled underneath. Their messy curls obscured more than half their face so that all Amos could see was their squished mouth.

"What you *should* do is get back to bed," Amos told them. "Potato soup isn't exactly a two-man job."

"I feel fucking useless." Joel peeled their face up and set their elbows on the table, sweeping back their hair. "If God was real, he'd let me die."

"Don't say that too loudly." Amos flicked a potato shred at them. It landed on the floor and Baron swept it up.

"Right." Joel coughed again. The harsh gust wracked their poor, tiny shoulders and they groaned in the aftermath. "Okay. Bed might not be such a bad idea."

Amos nodded his agreement and began plopping handfuls of sliced potatoes into a boiling broth. Baron ducked under the table and wiggled his way underneath Joel's feet, which was the dog's quieter way of making sure everyone knew that Jonah was about to walk in.

"Hey," Jonah yawned. Five in the afternoon, and he was just now stumbling downstairs. He wore a black satin robe that stopped mid-thigh and did nothing to conceal the fact that there was no underwear beneath.

"You're just in time for dinner," Amos said dryly. Jonah licked his lips and pulled a carton of milk from the fridge.

"Zee needs a ride to the church," Jonah said. "He has a meeting with the pastor. I'll probably grab something while we're out."

"I'm sure you will," Joel said. They couldn't keep the snark out of their voice.

Jonah shot them a look and popped open the carton's corner to drink the milk straight.

"Zee's feathers are all ruffled over that pop-up revival tent," Jonah said. "He gave me a righteous earful on the way to Jerry's house last night."

"Something tells me that Jerry isn't equally worried," Amos said. Jonah shrugged.

"Jerry won't start worrying until he starts bleeding attendance," Jonah reasoned. "But Zee keeps talking about omens and how it will all begin again with a tremble."

"Hmph--!" Joel coughed again and folded their arms on top of the table so they could rest their head. Jonah raised a red eyebrow and took another swig of milk.

"Something must be going around," he said. "Guy at the Super Value sounded just like that."

"Changing seasons," Joel muttered. "Cooling down." They coughed again. "Fall is my favorite time of year, yet look at what it does to me."

"Yeah, you look awful," Jonah said. "I think you should go lay down."

Joel shot the younger man a withering look. "I think I'll die here on the table," they said. "I want to make sure that I'm in the way while you're all trying to eat dinner."

Jonah laughed and replaced the milk carton in the fridge, grabbing an orange of unknown date or origin and punching his nail through the rind.

"Come on, Joel," he said. He peeled back the orange rind in uneven, ragged bits and tossed them towards the wastebasket. "You know, I heard today that the preacher they have down at the revival tent healed some woman's eyesight. Maybe you could go down there if you're not going to see a doctor."

"Is that what happened?" Amos shot Jonah a sarcastic look. "What junkie down at the Hole-n-Blow corner did you hear that from?"

Jonah scrunched up his forehead and grabbed a knife to slice up his orange. "It came from your mother. I saw her there."

"Shut up," Joel groaned. "Both of you. I mean, come on, Amos. At least snake oil preachers are free."

"Yeah," Amos said. "If you don't count the cost of each braincell you lose while listening to them minister." He held up his knife, pointing the tip at Joel, stern rather than threatening. "I don't trust anyone to lay hands on you and toss you around like a hacky-sack in the name of Christ, or miracle healing, or whatever. You'll have some soup, take some medicine, and you'll feel like a million bucks after a good night's sleep."

"As long as it's not *eternal* sleep." Jonah stuck the remaining bit of orange in his mouth. "If you change your mind though, Joel, I'll give you a ride."

"I'll remember that. You mean I get the choice between dying at the kitchen table *or* in your car?" They sighed and coughed again. "Lucky, *lucky* me."

# CHAPTER SIXTEEN

**E**zra's toothbrush was dangling out of his mouth and *I Dream of Jeannie* was playing on the television when his phone rang. He scrambled all the way to the kitchen to get it, socks sliding across the linoleum as he dove to answer.

Ezra cradled the phone between his ear and his shoulder as he hopped up on the counter to continue brushing his back teeth while talking at the same time. "Huwwo?"

"Hey, Ezra," Faye's voice on the other end was unmistakable. "What are you doing right now?"

Ezra rotated and spat into his kitchen sink. "Brushing my teeth," he said. "Getting ready to go to bed. Why?"

"It's only seven-thirty," she said.

"It's been a bad pain day," he shrugged even though she couldn't see him.

"Oh, I'm sorry." She paused, and then, "So I guess you don't want to come to revival with me, tonight?"

"You're going back?" For some reason, that thought was enough to turn his stomach. Ezra stuck his toothbrush back into his mouth to chew anxiously on the bristles.

"Yeah, I mean, I just think that I got a lot out of it." Faye's breath crackled against the receiver. "I guess I want to know if it was real or just a fluke."

"I dunno, Faye." Ezra rubbed the back of his neck. "My mobility hasn't been really good since this morning. Maybe you can get Chris to go with you?"

"He went home. He was hacking up a lung."

"Oh, man. Bless him."

"Yeah. Well, it's okay, then. I'll let you get some rest. I hope you feel better."

"Thanks." Ezra shifted on the counter, trying to ease some of the pain in his hips while they wrapped things up. "I'll leave the door unlocked for you. Pot roast is in the crockpot."

"Okay." She paused, like she was going to say something else.

"Be safe." He filled in the silence on his own. It was hard not to drop an 'I love you' over the phone. It was at least habit, maybe more. He wondered if that was her problem, too. Maybe they were both holding back the same shared, expired sentiment.

She hung up first, and he followed suit. Ezra transferred his toothbrush to his cheek and hopped down from the counter to go finish his ritual in the bathroom.

hen the phone rang again, it pulled Ezra out of a dead sleep. He had fallen asleep on the couch and now re-runs of *The Andy Griffith Show* were playing. His back and shoulders screamed at him as he sat up, and he rolled his neck to try and work out some of the kinks while plodding towards the kitchen.

He almost slipped and fell, forgetting he was wearing socks. Ezra grabbed his phone and leaned against the wall, pushing his fingertips into the corners of his eyes to try and chase out the heavy, all-consuming sleep that had settled there.

"Mhm?" He murmured into the receiver. "Hello?"

"Is this Ezra Buchanan?" This time, the voice on the other end was not one he got to hear very often. But Ezra would have known Mabel's voice if it had called out to him in the middle of a hurricane.

The realization of who it was woke him up a little bit.

"Yeah," Ezra said. "I mean, yes, this is he."

"It's Mabel Buchanan," she said. "I'm sorry to call you so late."

"Oh, it's no problem." Ezra glanced over at his kitchen clock and squinted. It was only just past 9PM. "What's wrong? Is everything okay?"

"Oh, good," she sounded relieved. "You were the only person I could think of to look up. There's a phone book here but I...anyway, I'm so sorry. My tire blew and I had to get the car towed, so now I'm stuck here at the garage and..."

"I can be there in no time." Ezra didn't even hesitate. "Which garage? O'Donnell's?"

"Yes," she said. "I can't thank you enough. Really."

"It's no trouble at all," he reassured her. "Just let me get dressed and I'll be out the door. I can be there in ten, fifteen minutes tops."

"You're a lifesaver," she breathed. Ezra swallowed hard.

"Don't mention it," he said. When he hung up the phone, he was blushing.

He hadn't even thought to ask about why she had called him and not either of her parents. It wasn't important, he supposed. Because she had called *him*. Mabel knew he could be trusted. He was *dependable*.

Ezra pulled on a pair of pajama pants and threw a t-shirt on over his binder. He doubled up by putting on a jacket, despite the sticky heat, and jumped into a worn pair of sandals before taking off.

He remembered to leave the door unlocked, but that was the only thought he intentionally gave towards Faye.

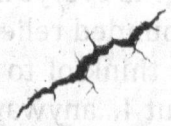

**M**abel Calhoun was waiting for him in the garage parking lot underneath a buzzing yellow lamp. She flagged him down with a wave and a smile, although she looked as exhausted as he'd ever seen her. When she got into the car, she dropped a plastic bag onto the floorboard along with her purse.

"I am so sorry about this," she said.

"It's really no trouble," he told her. "Do you want me to take you home?"

"No," her smile turned wry, "but I suppose you ought to."

"I don't have to." He started circling the parking lot while they figured out their plan. "Is there somewhere else you'd like to go?"

"I don't know," she said. "I just don't want to be home. My dad is over at the church and my mom will have *plenty* to say when she finds out that I blew a tire."

"It's not like you could help it," Ezra said. "Or like you did it on purpose."

"I know," Mabel sighed. "But it's her car."

Ezra winced. "Eugh," he said. "Well, have you eaten?"

"I would love something to eat. A burger and a shake, maybe," Mabel said. "It'll be my treat, since you were so kind as to pick me up."

"I wasn't doing anything, anyway," Ezra said, flicking on his turn signal before rubbing the back of his neck in embarrassment. "I was at home watching old TV shows. That's how I spend my time when I'm not at church." Never mind that his hips were on fire and his spine felt like it was on the verge of telescoping. If he just focused on driving and on the conversation, he could keep the pain on the back burner just a little bit longer.

"Don't you have a job?" Mabel asked. She moved the plastic bag around with her feet and shuffled like she was trying to get comfortable.

"I used to," Ezra replied. "I worked at the Super Value for a while until I couldn't anymore."

He could feel her eyes on him, even if he couldn't see her very well in the darkness.

"Did something happen?" she asked. "Were you injured?"

"No," he said. He never really knew how to answer that question, although plenty of people had asked. "It just—happened—one day. I mean, I've always had *some* pain, but I just thought it was all part of the retail-worker package. Then one day I couldn't stand up without pain shooting up my back and down my leg. I made it through my shift, but the next morning I couldn't move. I was in bed for...a week, I think. And since then, I haven't been able to go back to work."

"And the doctors haven't said anything about what it could be?"

Like he could afford a doctor. "No," he said. "They haven't been able to figure it out."

"Oh. So, how do you live?"

"Unemployment, mostly, and I'm lucky enough to live in my grandparents' old house. No rent." The words came out a bit drier than he meant them. Not because he was ungrateful, but because after he inherited the house, his parents stopped speaking to him altogether. It seemed like that had been their final straw.

"That is lucky," Mabel agreed.

It was seconds after Ezra pulled into the diner parking lot that he realized he had forgotten his crutch. He hadn't really anticipated *going* anywhere, so he must have left it by the door. It would be okay—he did not *technically* need it just to walk, but it was going to hurt like a bitch when he finally had a chance to stretch out on his bed. It was great timing, though, after he had just given that whole spiel about being too disabled to work.

He opened the door for Mabel and she smiled at him as she stepped out. Ezra's heart skipped a beat and he looked away quickly.

"What's in the bag?" he asked to distract himself.

"Oh," she hesitated. "It's um, medicine for my dad."

"Aw." Ezra shut the door behind her. "Something's been going around."

"Absolutely," she agreed quickly. Ezra tucked his hands into his jacket and started walking towards the diner, nudging that door with his shoulder to hold it open for her as well.

"You're such a gentleman," she teased.

"I try," he smiled.

"You succeed," she said. "I wish that you were..." She paused, round eyes getting a little wider as she caught herself mid-sentence. She moved past him quickly, trying to brush over the awkward moment, and that wave of bitterness he was so used to tasting came back.

She didn't have to finish. Ezra knew what she was going to say.

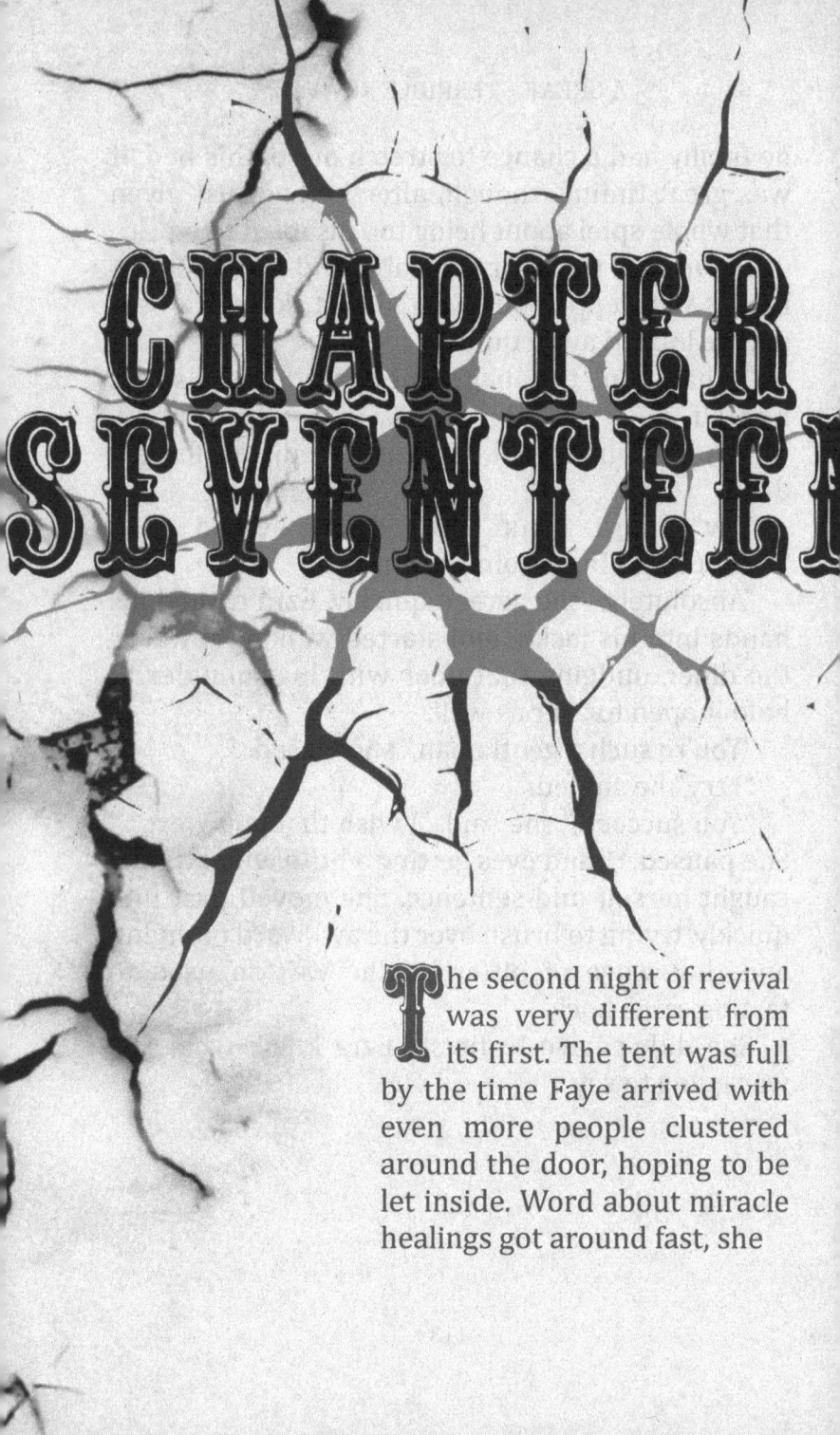

# CHAPTER SEVENTEEN

The second night of revival was very different from its first. The tent was full by the time Faye arrived with even more people clustered around the door, hoping to be let inside. Word about miracle healings got around fast, she supposed. She could have blamed Sweet Providence for its size, but there were plenty of faces she didn't recognize. Out-of-towners, for all she knew.

The crowd made her wish that she had taken the time to go home, change out of her work clothes, and freshen up a bit. In fact, the longer she stood there, the more ridiculous she felt.

Someone touched her arm, and Faye jumped. It took everything she had to just look over her shoulder and not bring her elbow up to jab the offender in the ribs. Of course, when she saw Fred Presley's face, she wished that she had been a little less restrained.

"Don't look so glad to see me," Fred snickered. Faye yanked her arm away.

"I'm lucky not to throw up, seeing you," Faye said. "Don't touch me."

"Here for some healing?" Fred asked. He snuck around her side with his head ducked like she was going to swing at any second. Probably a smart move. Meanwhile, he just looked like a skulking evil advisor.

"No, I'm not sick," Faye said. "I don't know why I'm here, actually. I think I might turn around and go home."

"Back to Ezra's house, you mean?" Fred smirked.

"Yes," Faye said shortly. "Back to Ezra's."

"You must not know what they're saying about you, Fay Wray."

115

"Shut up with that—what are you talking about?" She ground her teeth.

"Sarah Goody-Good Greenory has it out at for you down at the Cabinet. She's telling everyone about your..." he grinned and ducked his head even lower, scraping his nails over the back of his already-inflamed neck. "C-R-A-B-S-!"

"My what? My c-r-a...?" She paused to process his words, and then there was so much blood in her face that she felt like she was going to pass out. "Fuck that bitch!" She flung the words out a little *too* loudly, maybe, because several heads turned to stare at her.

"Shhh!" Fred pressed both hands against his mouth and guffawed through his fingers. "It's okay, Daisy-May-Fay. They make creams for that..."

"If you don't shut up, I'm going to hit you so hard your bottom teeth will be in your nose." Despite her threats, all the fight had left her body. All she wanted to do was crawl into a hole and disappear. It was embarrassing enough that the rumor existed, period. It was absolutely humiliating to have that news delivered to her through *Fred.*

Faye took a deep breath. "I don't have *crabs.*" She hissed the final sibilant through her teeth.

"Maybe *you* don't." Fred shook his head. "But more than half the Cabinet does."

"Well, that's probably because Jerry..." She bit the tip of her tongue before she said too much. "I'm going home."

Fred's hot, sweaty hand latched onto her wrist.

116

"Come inside," he said. "You're already here."

"If you don't stop touching me..."

"I saved you a seat. We're right in the belly of the beast."

It was odd wording, but Faye had learned by now that any answers would probably make less sense than the statements themselves. She let Fred weave through the tightly packed people in front of them and followed at his heels. He led her to the aisle seat where he had slung a ratty backpack and Faye stepped past him, taking the aluminum chair next to his. From there, they had a good view of the red-stained pulpit. It reminded her of a big, wide tongue.

When the reverend walked into view, the entire tent erupted with cheering. The reverend did not once smile. He did not smirk, he did not even glance in the direction of the gathered attendants. He sat down at his keyboard and began playing *'Victory in Jesus'.*

The crowd quieted down, but nobody sang. It was like they were all waiting for someone else to take up the mantle and lead. The reverend did not let out a sound. Faye looked around, trying to read every face for a sign—any sign—that the unbearable tension would soon be broken.

Salvation was nowhere in sight. Faye took a deep breath and began to sing.

*"Oh vic-to-ry, in Je-sus, my sav-ior, for-ever..."* she kept looking around as she sang, hoping it would encourage someone else to jump in.

Fred was the next to join, his scratchy baritone plucking at her eardrums in the same grating way it used to do every Sunday. *"He sought me, and he bought me..."*

*"With his redeeming blood!"* More voices joined in until a full chorus had formed. Faye found herself close to tears, but more from relief than being moved by the Spirit.

Reverend Grievance finally smiled. His grim purple mouth made a long line from one ear to the other like the cleave of a plum.

After a few Gospel hymns, Grievance abandoned the keyboard to stand behind the pulpit. The way he loomed, with his shoulders hunched and head lowered, made him look like an old buzzard sitting on a stump.

"Let's talk blood today, church," Grievance said. "More specifically, let's talk His Redeeming Blood. We all know the song, but what does it mean? How does it differ from the blood that runs through your veins? I think we all know that the blood of Jesus is everlasting and pure. It has the power to cleanse sins and wash away wrongs as if they had never been done."

His violet eyes settled on Faye, and her heart froze mid-thump.

"There are many hearts in this ol' world who could use a vigorous scrubbing with the blood of the Lamb. But there are a few untouched and precious souls who may yet serve as the vessels." He extended his hand, and it was almost as if his fingers were brushing against Faye's cheek. "Maybe you could be such a vessel."

Faye tried to breathe, but her lungs felt frozen, too. Everything was still. She couldn't even hear the blood rushing in her ears. There were only those violet eyes, and that kind, elderly face. The face of a grandfather she never had, full of warmth and affection. He was reaching out to her, and if she took his hand, then everything was going to be okay.

"All you have to do," the reverend said, "is ask 'Lord, what must I do to serve you?'"

"Lord..." Faye's voice trembled weakly. "What must I do to serve you?"

"This is how healing begins." The reverend beckoned her forward. Faye stumbled leaving her seat. She didn't even look down to see what she tripped on. Her vision had become so narrow. The gathered crowd had become a faceless blur—Christmas lights from a distance. She only saw the reverend and his outstretched hand. "Those who do not repent, those who turn their face away from the Endless Light, will be struck with boils and plague so that their blood...their hideous, fouled blood can heal the ones who truly deserve to live again."

Faye was within inches of the pulpit. She finally reached out and touched the reverend's hand and his fingers grasped hers. He pulled her forward, and for just one moment, it felt like she was floating.

"Do you believe that the Lord can use anyone?" the reverend asked.

"I do," she said.

"Do you believe that the Lord can use you?"

"I do."

"This is how healing begins." The reverend plastered his hand against her forehead and grasped her shoulder. "Come forward, church, as new prophets and priests are anointed so shall the Almighty work through their hands. Tell them your name, child."

"It is Faye," she said. She could barely speak. Tears rose, unbidden, and stung the back of her eyes. She didn't even know why she was crying. Her body did not feel as though it was hers, anymore. It was much lighter, as if her spirit was floating towards the top of the tent.

"Louder, so they all can hear you."

"It is Faye! Faye Warren!" She practically screamed it the second time around.

"Faye, will you serve the Lord?"

"Always, always." She was back to sobbing.

"Will you serve as the hand of Death?"

"I will do anything that I have to." She clutched her chest. There were so many hands on her, touching her shoulders, her back, and her head. She could feel them all at once, sweaty and trembling and so very hot.

*She* was so very hot. She could barely breathe. And still, she was floating.

"Sister Faye, the Lord will guide you to heal, as Death will guide you to devour." The reverend's words brought her back down. She was no longer floating. She was being pulled steadily towards the ground, a fish being reeled in on a line. Down, down, until she was back in her own skin, and her shoes were as heavy as lead.

Faye collapsed to her knees. She pressed her forehead against the dirt floor and couldn't bring herself to move. Her stomach quivered and she was in danger of vomiting, but even forcing herself to look up was an impossible task.

"God loves you, Faye Warren," Reverend Grievance said.

Warm, kind. *Loving.* Tender. His voice was a warm hug, the only thing that could stop the room from spinning.

"I know," she said softly.

"We love you, too." He touched her shoulders again, and she finally looked up. He was kneeling in front of her, and his eyes were so youthful and bright. "Look at all this family you have."

"My family..." Faye looked around. There was not a face in the crowd she could discern. Fuzzy Christmas lights. "My family."

# CHAPTER EIGHTEEN

**H**ezekiah's dreams were of Judgment Day and the skies were full of angels. They were Thrones, more specifically. Even in his dreams, he could differentiate them from the Archangel. They came down in the form of giant gold overlapping rings, each band covered in a multitude of eyes that blinked out of unison and rolled in separate directions. They flew over his house, spinning like UFO's, sheltered in darkness with the exception of thin threads of lightning that opened up the sky.

In his dreams, the agony was fresh. His skin never stopped burning. All he could smell was smoldering meat.

It was the smell that woke him up. The frightening imagery was all business-as-usual, but the nausea was uncomfortable enough to yank him back to consciousness. Hezekiah rolled over onto his good side and pushed himself up onto his elbow. The sheets beneath his hips were soaked in sweat. He reached out and looped his fingers through the plastic handle of his water cup before bringing it to his lips. There wasn't much sensation left in his fingers, so the handle kept him from dropping the cup altogether. However, his arm was already tired from taking on the burden of exerting extra effort to hold itself up, and his scarred shoulder ached.

Amos stirred against his back. Hezekiah huffed in soft irritation and gulped down another swallow of tepid water.

"What is wrong, Zee?" Amos asked in that deep, sleepy voice. Testosterone had been good to him in ways that Hezekiah and Joel could still only dream about, despite every one of them being on the same dose.

"It is nothing," Hezekiah murmured. "A dream."

On the other side of the wall, Joel coughed so hard that they gagged.

The covers moved and Hezekiah rolled back over. "Don't get up," he said.

Amos was already halfway to disobedience. "I'm just going to check on them," the red-haired man said. He rubbed at his bristly cheeks and swept a hand over his tired eyes. "They've been coughing like that all night."

"They should see a doctor," Hezekiah told him. "Have Jonah take them in the morning."

"I'll take them," Amos said. "Jonah's not home yet. I doubt they'll be getting up before noon."

Hezekiah sat up. Pain shot through his entire arm, but he didn't care. He found himself seeking out Amos' warm brown eyes in the darkness, but they were swallowed up along with the rest of his features. "What do you mean, Jonah isn't home yet?" he asked. "What is he out doing?"

Amos froze. Hezekiah took note of how his lover's broad shoulders tensed up.

"He just said he was going on a drive," Amos said. "I don't know, Zee. He does that sometimes."

"Hm." Hezekiah trailed his fingers down Amos' spine. His lover shivered while goosebumps popped up over the expanse of his bare flesh.

Hezekiah leaned over and dropped a kiss onto Amos' shoulder. "I don't need you getting sick, too."

"I don't *want* to get sick," Amos told him. "And I don't want you to get sick. God knows." He finally turned his face towards Hezekiah, brown eyes catching a little bit of the moonlight that poured in from the window behind their heads. "We both know that your entire immune system is on thin ice."

Hezekiah's lip curled, but he didn't answer. There were certain things about Amos he valued, and subsequently certain things that he tolerated as well. Hezekiah would never let someone like that tool Jerry talk about his susceptibility to disease or pain, but Amos *knew* him.

Amos was the one who had picked him up after the lightning strike. Amos was the one who had carried him to bed when the scars that bloomed across his shoulder like tangled fungus roots were raw and red and too painful to bear.

"We will see how things are in the morning," Hezekiah said. "Get a little bit more sleep."

Amos nodded. He didn't need much convincing, on that front. He laid back down and Hezekiah turned onto his good side, tucking his hand underneath his pillow.

He didn't go back to sleep. He stared at the wall all night and pondered.

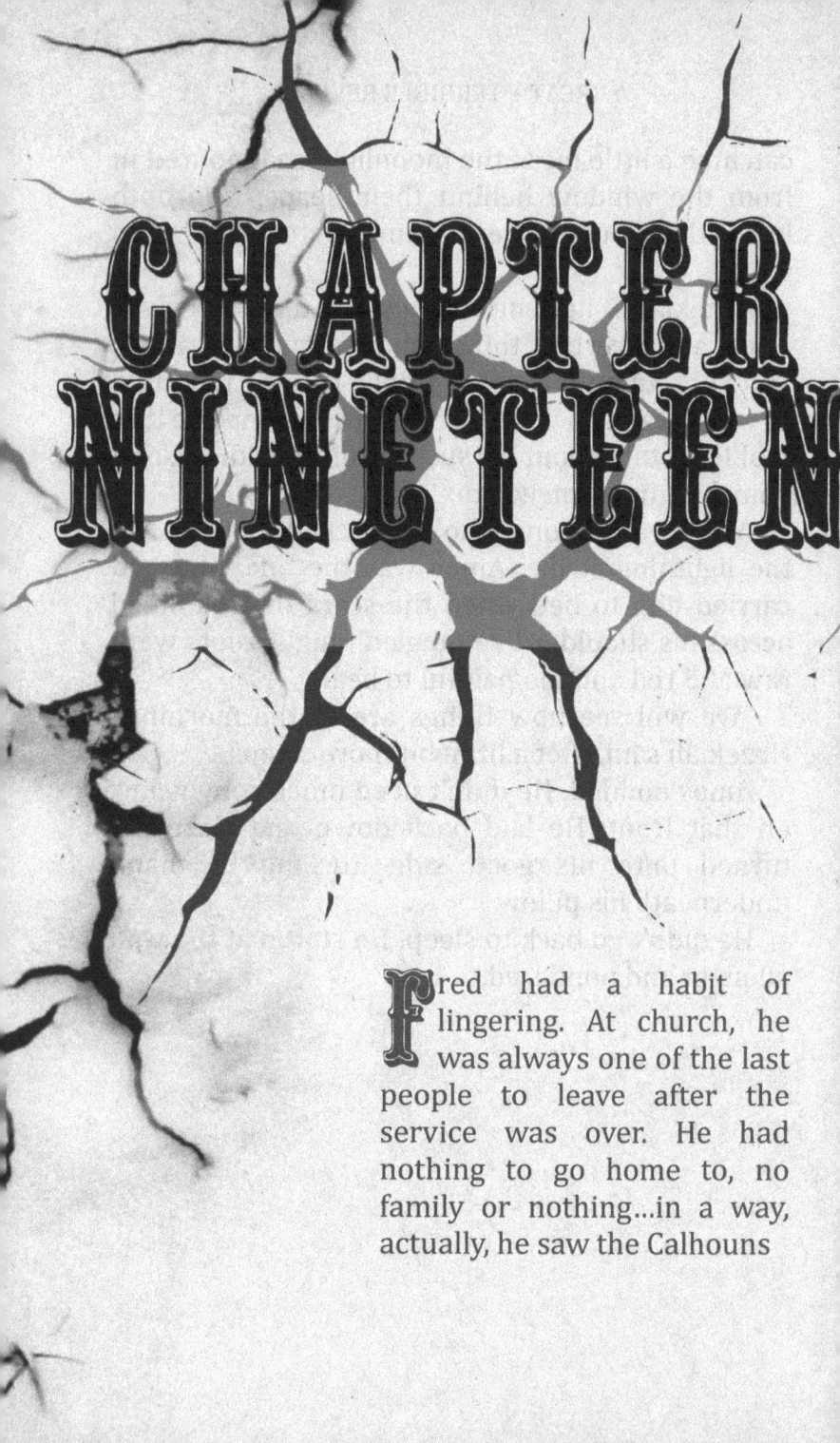

# CHAPTER NINETEEN

**F**red had a habit of lingering. At church, he was always one of the last people to leave after the service was over. He had nothing to go home to, no family or nothing...in a way, actually, he saw the Calhouns as his family. Jerry had this way of preaching that made Fred feel like he was being spoken to directly, even all the way from the pulpit. And Isabel always made sure to give him a special little Christmas or Easter bag whenever she was passing out Avon orders to all the church ladies. Then there was Mabel, who was sweeter than apple pie and always had a kind word to say to Fred when she passed him in the hallway. The apple of Jerry's eye. So sweet-smelling and soft-spoken that it was impossible to believe she wasn't married yet.

Fred figured he might have a shot at courting her himself, if no one else stepped up to the plate. She was going on twenty and that was a long time for a young woman to wait. He just had to figure out how he was going to ask for Jerry's blessing.

At revival, Fred found himself lingering even though there was no Mabel or Isabel to talk to when everyone else had wandered away. Habit, he would wager, more than anything. After watching Faye disappear into the crowd, he caught himself wandering around the edges of the tent until he finally meandered over to the entrance. By then, the last of the attendants were saying their goodbyes out in the dry Texas grass.

A few clouds rolled past the sliver of moon and teased rain, but it was likely an empty promise.

'WHAT'S THAT?' the imp's shriek was so out of the blue that Fred jumped and smacked the side of his head, hissing to let out his anger.

"There's nothin'!" he growled. "What the hell are you talking about?"

*'The ground is shaking!'* the imp's leathery wings beat against the inside of his skull. They scraped against the bone and left Fred moaning in pain. *'Can't you feel that? Idiot!'*

"Fred Presley. Do I have that right?" The voice that had become increasingly familiar to him cut through the blinding curtain of pain and smothered the imp's screams. Fred froze with one arm raised. When he looked underneath it, he saw the tall, grim reverend standing behind him with his pinched bird-face half-obscured in shadow.

Reverend Grievance looked exactly like a buzzard, minus the hooked beak. He had a wrinkled red head and black, beady eyes peering out from underneath hard, deep ridges. When he spoke, his teeth were white and sharp like bone shards.

Fred should have been scared, but he wasn't. The imp *was* scared, and there was satisfaction in the tormentor being the tormented for a change of pace.

"Yessir," Fred breathed, rotating on his heel to face the reverend. "Fred Marshall Presley." He clacked his teeth and stuck out his hand. The reverend didn't take it, but the old man smiled at him, the entire expression contained in a single thin line.

"I had been hoping that we could have a moment to talk," the reverend said. "I've heard that you've got quite the testimony."

128

'*The ground is shaking,*' the imp continued to whisper while Fred tried to hold his wits together. '*It's going to open up right under our feet. It's going to swallow us whole, goddamn you, idiot—! Pay attention!*'

"I do," Fred managed to push the words out. "I like to think so, rather. Testimony is important. There're young people all over who don't know about Jesus and don't know how close they are to seeing the fires of Hell."

'*Old turkey-face. Old bone-cruncher. Smells like dead meat.*' The imp turned in circles and Fred flinched in pain.

The grim reverend extended his hands. Fred flinched again as ice-cold fingers touched the sides of his head. The reverend traced his fingertips along the harsh mound of scarred, stapled flesh that protruded from Fred's scalp. It didn't hurt, but it was an odd feeling. So much of the strangeness came from the fact that Fred still wasn't used to any place on his head being bare.

When the reverend touched him, the imp immediately quieted. Its mumblings were reduced to discontented growls and it settled, curling back around his stem where it usually sat. Fred let out a small groan in relief. Its needle-like talons were still digging into his brain meat, but he could handle that.

"Is that better?" the reverend asked. Fred nodded and the reverend continued to stroke his temples, scratching his thick nails along the dip of Fred's nape.

"Why don't you share your testimony with me?" the reverend asked. "I am very keen on hearing it." As he spoke, he swirled his thumbs over Fred's skin, working them into the base of his skull and smoothing out the tight muscles.

Fred cleared his throat. He had shared his testimony over a dozen times, it felt like, but never before had it been so difficult to get started. "Well, I don't rightly know where to begin."

"At the very start of things." The reverend pushed his fingers in deeper until the muscles twinged. "Were you raised Christian?"

"Yes, sir," Fred sighed and closed his eyes. "Mama was a God-fearing woman and my father was too. Every time the church doors were open, they had me and my two brothers out there praising God."

"Then what happened?"

Fred licked his lips. "Beer," he said. "Beer, whiskey, and cigarettes...poker...reckon I lost almost sixty grand in one year on poker. Left home, came here, couldn't keep a job, couldn't feed my habit. I was wanderin' around, not really living life. Wasn't happy at all, I *knew* there was something missing." A wire of tension pulled every muscle in his body taut, and it was all he could do to fight against going rigid. The reverend's fingers helped, making deep, small circles that left Fred's neck and shoulders limp. But his arms ached, and he had to rub them to keep himself grounded. The dry,

130

peeling skin around his nail beds itched and he had to fight not to start gnawing.

"When you talk about it, do you relive it?" the reverend asked.

"Sometimes," Fred admitted. "Not sure why. I've told this story a hundred times."

A squeal of pain echoed from the deepest, meatiest part of his brain and set a spike of agony up to his crown. Fred ground his teeth ducked his head, trying to bring up his hand to slam it into the side, to quiet the imp and distract from his own suffering at the same time.

The reverend caught his hand and started rubbing Fred's wrist until the tendons were loose and his palm felt like it was being pricked by a dozen needles.

"Hold your focus," the reverend said gently. "What brought you back to the Lord?"

Fred swallowed hard and closed his eyes. "I was driving down Verrutuck Road and going way, way too fast. I was drinking all the time, at that point. I'd buy a Big Gulp, fill it halfway with Coke, finish that, and then fill it back up with a tall boy while peeling down the highway. I saw a—well I *thought* I saw a deer, and I swerved, but then I hit the damn thing and its guts burst all over my windshield and I went *flying* right into the nearest tree. Nearly flipped my damn car, too—it was all quicker than lightning. But when I tell you, reverend...the next thing I knew was I woke up in Hell. And it was just as bad as mama told me it would be. It was pitch-black and *hot.* My eyeballs were swimming in my own sweat and I couldn't see my own hand in front of my face. And all I could hear were screams." The memory turned his stomach. "I've never—never heard such screams in all my life, reverend. Like coyotes being skinned alive."

"That must have been terrifying." The reverend's cool, sympathetic tone was the single, tenuous thread that kept Fred grounded.

"I cried," Fred admitted. "I fell to my knees and I was sobbing like a wretch, begging for God to save me. I promised all kinds of things, like I would never drink again and I would start going back to Church. He..." The next part he always amended, which felt like a sin in as of itself, but it barely sounded real even to him. Fred always told it as the Lord reached down His hand and pulled His lost, wretched lamb out of the mouth of Hell itself. Then Fred woke up— easy, plain and simple.

Except now, standing with the reverend, the truth was being pulled from his mouth on a long string—and he could not stop it. He was practically vomiting it out.

The grim reverend's fingernails were digging into the back of his head. Seeking, scraping. It didn't hurt, but Fred heard every single scratch.

"An angel came to me," Fred heaved. "He appeared in golden armor and carried a flaming sword. He told me, *'Fred Presley, from now on you will neither speak nor hear any word against God'.* He put a fat white worm to my ear and I heard it

132

*wriggle* inside. It ate its way into my brain and it hatched into that greasy little imp. And then...then I woke up. I was in a hospital, and the doctors there told me there had never been any deer—then whose guts were all over my windshield? They never gave me an answer to that."

"A whole life without answers," the reverend said. "That is what leads so many men astray."

"Yeah." Fred rubbed his arms at last while the overwhelming desire to go home hit him like a freight train. Suddenly, the grim reverend seemed less grandfatherly, and more like a moving wax effigy. That turkey-red face began to fade into a greyer, human-shaped blob, and Fred's heart rate kicked up to double its pace.

"Well, look at that." The reverend's knobby fingers held up something in front of Fred's nose and he leaned forward, squinting to try and bring it into focus. It looked like a struggling white grub. It flailed back and forth, arching over the reverend's fingertips in every direction until he squeezed its round middle and it popped in half like a zit, oozing white and green pus all over his mottled skin.

"You are free, Fred Marshall Presley," the grim reverend told him. "Do with that what you will."

"What do you mean?" Fred rubbed his ear and the back of his head. There was a dime-sized hole in the nape of his neck, but the whole area still felt numb. When he pulled his hand back, it was covered in blood, and he was hit with a stink not unlike rotting fish.

The grim reverend said nothing else. He turned his blurry head and started walking away.

"Hey! Wait!" Fred took one step forward to try and follow but collapsed to the ground instead, landing hard on one knee.

A vulture landed beside him, cocking its head to one side and ogling him with one dark eye. Fred clenched his teeth and hissed at the bird, spitting in its direction when it didn't move.

"Stupid bird! Get away!" He groaned and held the back of his head, trying to stop the blood from trickling down his neck. "I'm not dead, you fuck. Go find dinner somewhere else!"

The bird hopped forward, continuing its hard stare. Fred shouted and kicked one foot out, wiggling his boot in the air to make as much of a threat as possible. The vulture finally flew away, but the sudden movement knocked him back, and Fred lay on the grass for a full minute before trying to get back up, just staring at the sky.

The last of the cars had gone, and the world was upsettingly quiet.

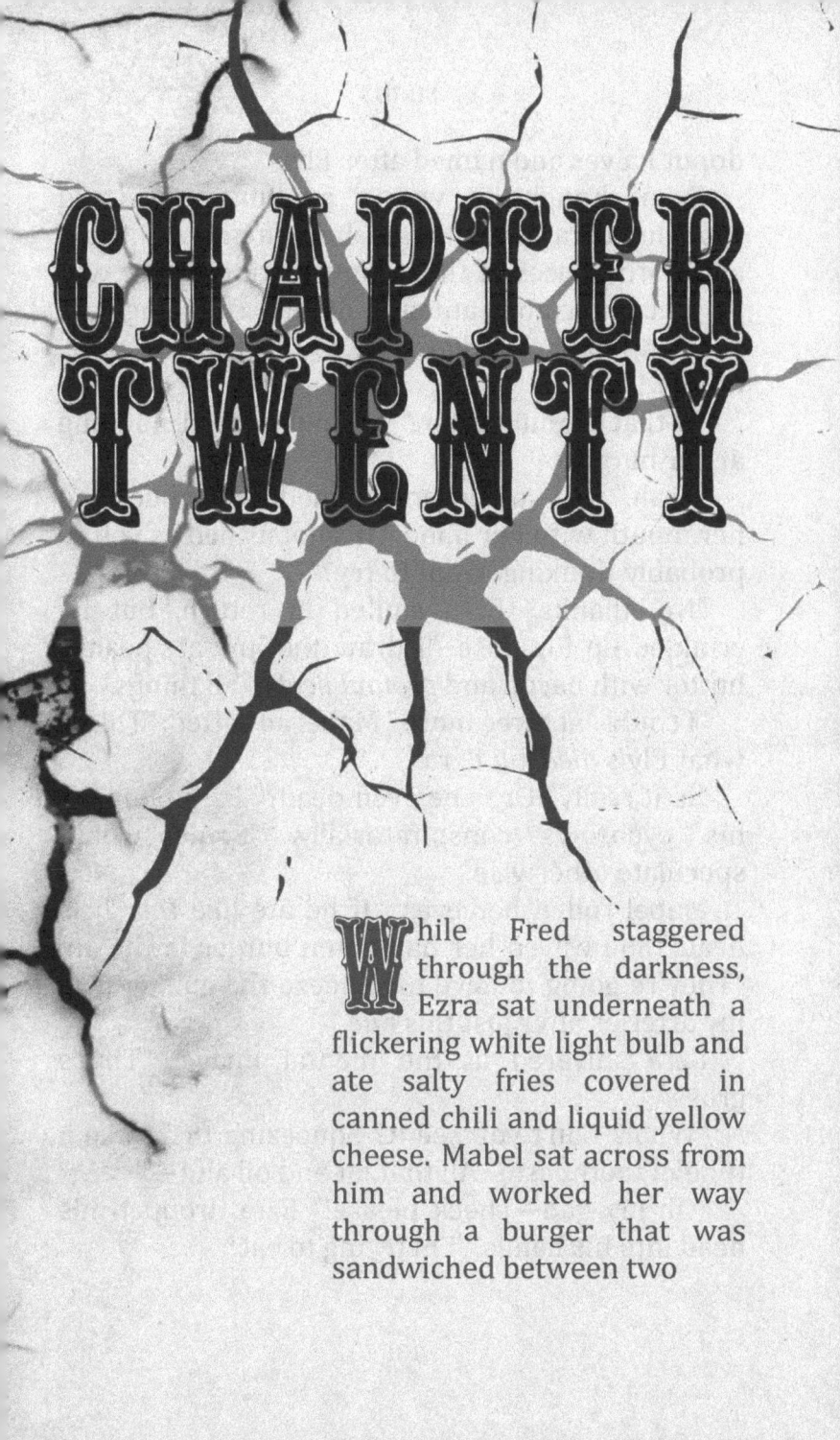

# CHAPTER TWENTY

While Fred staggered through the darkness, Ezra sat underneath a flickering white light bulb and ate salty fries covered in canned chili and liquid yellow cheese. Mabel sat across from him and worked her way through a burger that was sandwiched between two donut halves and named after Elvis.

Even though he wasn't as hungry as he'd thought, Ezra was glad to have food to fill any awkward pauses in their conversation. There was an uncomfortable amount of dry coughing and sneezing in the background to do fill that space, otherwise.

"Is that peanut butter?" he finally asked, nodding at her burger.

"Yeah." She smiled and immediately concealed her mouth with her hand. "It's not as bad as you're probably thinking. Want to try?"

"No, thanks." Ezra smiled in return, but he crinkled up his nose. "I draw the line at...peanut butter with bacon and *ground beef* of all things."

"I could eat three more," Mabel admitted. "This is what Elvis *died for,* Ezra."

"Is it really? Or is he even dead?" Ezra bounced his eyebrows conspiratorially. "Some would speculate otherwise."

Mabel rolled her eyes. "If he ate like *this,* he's dead." She waved her half-eaten burger in the air. "They're going to have to squeeze the gunk out of my arteries after just this *one.*"

Ezra shivered at the mental image. "That's gross."

"What? Can't you see it? Squeezing them like a tube of toothpaste? All that fat and oil and—"

"Oh my god—check please!" Ezra dropped his head into his hands. "I'm trying to eat."

Mabel giggled and dabbed at her face with a napkin. "Sorry," she said. "But you *are* really cute when you blush."

That only made his face warmer. Ezra weighed the pros and cons of keeping his nose only an inch from the table forever.

He finally lifted his head when dizziness started to creep in. At the same time, he caught a glimpse of Chris West walking up to the door through the window that sat just behind Mabel. Ezra raised his hand on instinct but then lowered it immediately, realizing he didn't *actually* want to engage with his old coworker.

Chris didn't seem to notice him, anyway. The man looked a little rough, with the bags under his eyes carrying the weight of his problems and his unwashed hair stuck in so many directions he resembled a plane propeller. He smothered a cough with his hand as he walked up to the register and Ezra watched the waitress behind it wince.

"One cup of black coffee and a Nana's Breakfast plate to-go..." Chris rasped. He coughed again into his hand before he could finish and turned away from the register to spare the waitress. Each dry, rattling gust sounded like his tongue was being dragged over a washboard and then tapered off into retching. He doubled over and panted, clutching his stomach with his tongue hanging out. The whole organ was dark purple, with spots of white freckling the surface like a deadly toadstool.

Ezra wanted to leave. He didn't even care about taking home his leftovers. His concern for Chris did not outweigh his desperation to be as far away from any type of plague as possible.

"Should we call someone?" Mabel whispered.

"I don't know," Ezra told her. Even as he spoke, Chris gripped the register and pulled himself up straight. His pale knuckles had wide, dark red splits along their creases.

"Thank you." Chris accepted a glass of water from the waitress and chugged the entire thing. There were at least half a dozen faces peering out through the cut-out kitchen window, exchanging dubious looks.

"One cup of black coffee and a Nana's Breakfast to-go." The waitress' voice was a bit shaky as she repeated his order. "$6.35. It'll be just a few minutes if you want to sit down..."

"I'll wait outside," Chris muttered. He fumbled with his jacket pocket and pulled out a pack of cigarettes as he turned back towards the door.

He glanced over and, for just half a second, Ezra locked gazes with him. Chris' eyes looked like they were swimming in blood.

"I'm going to check on him," Ezra said. Before Mabel could respond, he pulled himself up using the edge of the table and followed his former coworker outside. Every muscle in Ezra's lower back was tighter than a guitar string and the pain radiated down his left leg. The hard, scooped booth seating did him no favors.

He ground his teeth against the agony and found himself in the baked night air, standing on a crumbling cement sidewalk while Chris leaned against a window and coughed into his hands.

Ezra waited for him to finish, wishing he had something to cover his own mouth and nose. He kept a few steps' worth of distance between them and told himself that germs couldn't fling themselves that far.

When Chris finished his coughing fit, he shot Ezra a baleful look. His hands trembled as he lit his cigarette.

"What's up?" Chris asked. His voice was strained, and he grumbled like he was holding back another fit.

"Nothing," Ezra told him. "I just came out to check on you. Do you need a ride to the doctor or something?" He glanced over at Mabel through the window. "I just need to drop someone off real quick beforehand."

"Nah." Chris shook his head. "I'm good." He grumbled again and pressed his hand against his chest, pausing before he continued. "I just need to get some sleep."

"Yeah?" Ezra looked him up and down. "You look like you were left for dead on a riverbank."

Chris laughed. That cost him, and his cigarette went flying from his mouth as his lungs squeezed out another wheezing cough. "Fuck!" He clenched his teeth. "God—yeah, I feel like it too." He tried to pull in a deep breath, but it was clear he couldn't quite take a full one. "Donald scheduled me for back-to-back shifts all week. But I'm calling in tomorrow—fuck it."

"That sounds like a good idea," Ezra said gently. Chris produced another cigarette and then leaned back against the window. He let himself slide down until he sat on the sidewalk with his shoulders pressed against the side of the building. When he rubbed his face, something squelched.

"I'm here for you, man." Ezra's hip was screaming at him. "Do you still have my number?"

"Yeah, yeah." Chris puffed on his cigarette. "Thanks, man."

As much as he would have liked to, Ezra couldn't physically lift Chris off the sidewalk and haul him to the emergency room. After a few more seconds of hesitation, he walked back inside, pausing long enough to hold the door open for a waitress carrying a to-go bag.

"Did he say anything?" Mabel asked as soon as Ezra sat back down.

"Only that he's fine and he doesn't need me." Ezra shrugged. "I don't agree, but I guess I can't make him do anything."

"I guess not." Mabel glanced down at the plastic red basket her food had arrived in and tapped her fingers against the rim. "Do you want any dessert?"

"No." Ezra grabbed his glass to suck down the rest of his soda. "I think I'm ready to go home."

"Me too." Mabel grabbed the ticket sitting on the edge of the table. "Well, not really. But I think we should get out of here."

"Yeah." Ezra heard Chris' violent coughing's from the other side of the wall. "That's probably a good idea."

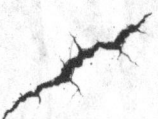

When they arrived at the pastor's house, Ezra made sure to turn off his headlights and park on the street so that he didn't disturb anyone inside. Mabel gathered up her things and sat for a whole minute with the plastic bag wedged between her legs, as if she was seriously considering not going in at all.

"Thank you for picking me up," she finally said. She looked over at Ezra and gave him the prettiest smile he had ever seen. His ears burned.

"No problem," he said. "Anytime."

Mabel leaned over and, quicker than Ezra could register, kissed his cheek. By the time he was able to process the moment, she had already slipped out of the car and shut the door.

Ezra touched his gear stick, but he didn't leave until he was sure that Mabel had made it safely inside.

# CHAPTER TWENTY-ONE

**F**ridays were for bank deposits. Then they were for hair appointments, facials, and shopping through the latest in JC Penney shoes and dresses. Isabel took her Fridays very seriously, because they usually determined the outcome of her Sunday—whether her perm would be set, whether her pantyhose would have runs, whether the diamond on her wedding ring would be polished. There was a lot of pressure in being Jerry's third (she never counted

herself second, not with Hezekiah Rampling in the picture). If her nail polish was chipped, if her hands were rough, if her skirt hem was frayed, then everything came back to him.

If he could afford to keep his wife up to the standards that the likes of Paula White had set, then that was a testimony to God's favor and gifts of abundance. In return, Isabel was expected to keep Jerry's suits pressed and his collars starched—which was never about money, but her role as the subservient housewife. An appointment as old as time.

In truth, Isabel couldn't even remember the last time she had ironed a pair of pants. These days, she sent everything off to the dry cleaner and put all her charges on a credit card. Prosperity, sure—as long as it could be paid off in installments.

Isabel flipped the red switch on her coffee pot and turned her attention towards tidying up the kitchen while it brewed. The smell of coffee alone was enough to lift her spirits, along with the trails of golden sunlight that poured in through the sliding glass door that led out onto the back porch. She spent so much time outside of it that she managed to forget how much she actually liked her house. It was a lot nicer and prettier when Jerry wasn't lumbering around.

There was a plastic bag crumpled on top of the stove and Isabel picked it up. It still had something in it, so she moved it to the kitchen table, but not before glancing inside.

A silver tube flashed, catching her attention from underneath the plastic folds. She fished it out of the bag, holding it by its white cap as she turned it around to glance at the bold blue word 'RID' on the front. Smaller, orange lettering underneath it read: *1% Permethrin. Kills lice within six days.*

Isabel choked on a sudden surge of disgust she could not articulate. The tube slipped out of her fingers and clattered against the floor, skittering underneath a kitchen chair. When she bent to pick it up, her daughter's voice floated over from the kitchen entrance.

"Good morning—oh." Mabel's realization followed right on the heels of her greeting. Isabel turned towards her daughter and held up the tube, letting her wordless question hang in the air with all the impending threat of an axe-headed pendulum.

"It isn't mine," Mabel said quickly.

When Isabel swallowed, her throat was full of knives. "Who is this for?" she demanded. She tried to keep her anger under control, but she could hear it eking out with every syllable. "Who do *you know* that is embroiled in such disgusting activities?" She had to force herself to spit out the last words. *Her daughter* had walked into a pharmacy and bought a tube of medicated cream for pubic lice. *Her daughter* had used *Jerry's* money—church money—to fund some degenerate's wayward lifestyle.

Isabel found herself gripping the tube so tightly that the top had started to bulge. Any tighter and it was in danger of popping off altogether.

"It's..." Mabel's pink tongue poked out between her lips as she took far too long to answer. "It's for Faye Warren." She cast her eyes down and her cheeks flushed bright red. "I thought that if she had—access to the medicine she needed—she might be able to return to the Cabinet."

Isabel's expression wrenched into one of disgust and she threw the tube back down into the bag. "Faye Warren does not need your help," she said. "She has dug her own grave and she can dig herself back out. I don't want you spending anymore money on that..." several words raced through her brain, none of them savory, "...*slut*. She must make the decision, the *right* decision, to turn back to God on her own time. Only then can she be healed. This sort of thing only enables her."

"I'm sorry," Mabel said quietly. Isabel blew out another hard breath through her nostrils.

"Your heart is in the right place," she said. "But *women* like Faye tend to make *men* like Ezra Buchanan." She shook her head. "And I think that we could do with fewer of those, all-around."

150

Mabel opened her mouth, but if she had anything to say, she kept it to herself. She bit the bottom corner of her lip and drew it in, extending her hand. "I have to tell you something," she said. "Before you go anywhere."

"What else could you possibly have to tell me?" Isabel wondered aloud.

She knew her daughter. Mabel had a habit of lying when she wanted to get out of trouble. When she was younger, she never had any trouble whipping up a couple of tears and sticking out her bottom lip for the sake of a lesser punishment. Now that she was a grown woman, it was harder for her to squirm out of uncomfortable situations. It was good for her to squirm, so Isabel let it happen. Somehow, Mabel had to learn that the real world did not care about her tears.

"Your car needs to be picked up from the shop." Mabel spoke her confession so quickly that all her words ran together. "I blew a tire while I was out last night and then I had to—get a taxi home. I'm sorry," she added quickly. "I know that's inconvenient."

While the news could have been worse, Isabel still could not help feeling irritated. "Yes," she said. "That *is* inconvenient, actually. Now you want me to take a taxi all the way down there so I can pick up my own car? That's not very responsible of you."

"I know," Mabel said. "I'm sorry."

"So, we'll owe the mechanic for, what? Towing it, I assume, and then keeping it overnight. Plus a new tire, and then the taxi you took, and the taxi I'm going to have to take. I'll be taking all of that from your monthly allowance, I hope you know that."

Mabel turned white, but she just nodded her acceptance. "I understand," she whispered.

Isabel wasn't sure if she actually wanted her daughter to scream at her, but she felt like it would be better than the meek acceptance. "Actually, this is what we are going to do," Isabel continued. "*You* are going to go pick the car up from the shop and then bring it back here. I am not going to rush out of here for an extra errand that is not my responsibility to take care of."

"Yes, ma'am," Mabel said. More meek resignation. It somehow came across as both spineless *and* mocking. Isabel wanted to slap her.

Mabel started to leave, then she paused to gesture at the bag Isabel had forgotten she was still holding. "I'll get that out of your way."

Isabel tossed the bag. Mabel caught it mid-air.

"I don't want you to bring that trash into my house ever again," Isabel said.

"I won't, mama," Mabel muttered.

# CHAPTER TWENTY-TWO

The chipped white sink was littered with three different hand soaps, all half-empty, and a thin dried-out white bar that had three other colored bars stacked on top of it to form one lump.

Jonah's head disappeared beneath all of them when he went to splash his face with water. The red spirals that corkscrewed from his scalp, shorter and more coppery than Amos' own, were pulled back so tightly that they left the edges of his scalp white.

When Jonah lifted his head, Amos flung a towel at him, only somewhat satisfied to see the dark terrycloth wrap around his metamour's neck.

"Joel needs to go to the doctor," Amos said. Jonah groaned.

"Can't you take them?" the younger man asked. "I just got back, and I haven't slept all night."

"Nope," Amos said. "Zee has Babylon Prayer today and actually needs someone to stay *with* him."

Jonah made a face. "I can stay with him," he said.

"And not fall asleep in the pew," Amos amended. "You're really bad at staying conscious when it matters."

Jonah pulled the end of the towel around and scrubbed his face. Under almost any other circumstances, Amos would have felt sorry for the guy. The rings under his eyes were numerous enough to count his age. Like a tree.

If only he made better choices.

"All right," Jonah said, defeated. "Which doctor? The one on Munich?"

"Yes," Amos told him.

"That's a good 40 minutes away. I'll need gas."

*'You wouldn't if you hadn't stayed out all night driving around,'* was what Amos wanted to say. Instead, he reached into his back pocket and pulled out his wallet.

"Make sure Joel eats, too," he said.

"I'll see what I can do." Jonah saluted.

Amos touched the doorknob to pull it shut. It buzzed a little in his hand, but he was too distracted to give it much attention.

# CHAPTER TWENTY-THREE

It started raining on the day of Babylon Prayer, which fell on every Friday and was the day Hezekiah and Jerry drank whiskey in the church sanctuary until Hezekiah started seeing visions. The prophet swore up and down that He never laced the spirit with anything extra. But if that was truly the case, then Jerry wanted to know how come Hezekiah was the one seeing angels and hearing the voice of God, while he was left to fend for himself thumbing through bible reference books on Saturday nights.

The two bottles of whiskey were already sitting out on the counter when Jerry walked into his kitchen. The smell of perfume and hairspray drifted down the hallway, leading to a triangle of yellow light that was enough to tell him that Isabel hadn't left yet.

A pang hit Jerry in the crotch and made him wince. Seemed like these days, every time he got a little bit of blood flowing down there, he ended up paying for even the thought of having an erection.

And it itched—*goddamn,* did it itch. Mabel was supposed to bring home something to help, but he was starting to think she had blown all the money he handed her on bubblegum and records.

Jerry shoved his hands down the front of his pants to try and soothe the itching with a little bit of pressure. Every time he scratched, it was like razors being dragged across his skin, but it was getting more and more tempting. He leaned against the wall and tried to get a glimpse of his wife through the open hall bathroom door. Isabel had taken that one over as her own, much like she had claimed the guest bedroom across from Mabel's, leaving Jerry on his own in the queen-size marital bed with nothing but rented skin flicks for company.

She claimed it wasn't anything personal. She said that his snoring triggered her migraines. And went it came down to the wire, she could either move rooms or waterboard him in his sleep.

Isabel stood in front of the bathroom sink, over a yard of golden legs and golden hair, all bombshell blond with hazy blue Bambi eyes and cracked pink lips that belonged on the cover of a magazine. She could have been a Bond girl, or the centerfold of *Playboy,* but she had married him instead. She was a lot of pent-up potential squeezed into nude 3-to-a-package pantyhose.

He caught her eyes in the mirror, and their corners immediately scrunched up. Even from where he was standing, he could see the deep lines of crow's feet.

"Good morning, Jerry," she said. There was nothing connubial or even cordial about her intonation. He might as well have been walking into a bank.

"Morning, Izzy," he said. She hated that nickname, but Hezekiah used it and now Jerry couldn't get it out of his head. "Where are you off to?"

"Well, Mabel just brought the car back. So, I am going to make the church deposit," she replied. "Then I am going to my hair appointment. Same as every Friday." Her chest rose with a sigh and then she asked, "Where are you going?"

"Down to the church," he said, "for Babylon Prayer." It felt more important to say it that way.

"How nice for you." She turned, and he caught a glimpse of her full glory. All these years together and she still took his breath away.

The itch came back, and he gave in to scratching. Her entire expression shifted into something closer to disgust.

"Really?" She scoffed. "Jerry."

"Sorry, Izzy," he mumbled. He really didn't want to explain how he couldn't help it. Somehow, that just sounded worse in his head. "You look nice."

She sucked on her teeth, as if she couldn't decide whether to take that as a compliment or not, and then turned off the bathroom light as she walked out.

"I don't want to be late for my appointment," she said.

"I don't want you to be late," he agreed.

"I'll be home after dinner." She spared only half a glance towards the kitchen. "You and Mabel might want to order something."

"I'll probably be home late, too."

"Well, then she can fend for herself. She's a big girl."

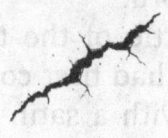

159

When Jerry finally arrived at the sanctuary, Hezekiah was already there. The prophet sat in a metal folding chair across from its empty twin, one leg crossed so that His ankle rested on the opposite knee. He looked like He was already on the edge of His trance, fingertips pressed into His temples, making little circles as they traveled from sockets to crown. The toe of His shiny black shoe spun through the air, swinging back and forth so that both His legs trembled.

Jerry caught sight of Amos, one of Hezekiah's redheads, but didn't bother with a greeting.

Jerry took his seat in the chair opposite the prophet and set one bottle of whiskey on the floor. He kept the other and turned it around in his hands, lingering over it for only a second before popping the cork and taking a swig. That first burn was the best. Good whiskey was like Listerine after biting your tongue. Jerry let it sit near the back of his mouth, holding it there until Hezekiah's eyes sprang open, and then he swallowed.

"Looks like you've already gotten started," Jerry said. He passed the bottle over to Hezekiah, who took it without a word.

There was so little of the teenager that Jerry used to know, who had first come to church in an olive-green dress with a satin-and-tulle skirt and called everyone 'sir' and 'ma'am'. That young'un had been scrubbed off the face of the earth—taken out back and shot by whatever had become Hezekiah in her place.

Jerry liked to think that he wasn't prejudiced. He was tolerant, after all, where a lot of pastors were not. He let Ezra Buchanan and Faye Warren and even Amos Sleyde walk around—and he never treated them any different. As long as they minded their own business, as long as they remembered their place and didn't try to overturn the natural pecking order within the congregation—that was all Jerry really asked of anyone.

With Hezekiah, however, there was a good deal *not* to like. Hezekiah had designs, He thought real highly of Himself and of His relationship with God. It was all there before the lightning strike, the self-importance and sharp scrutiny, but the lightning drew it to the surface. The silver scars that dribbled down from His jawbone to His collar were the cracks in His veneer that no amount of knotted flesh could seal back up.

And that molded, disgusting marble that roamed around its socket, looking every way but forward while the pretty one stayed fixed, staring Jerry down like it could see straight through to his throbbing heart. If Jerry squinted and put all his focus on only half of Hezekiah's face, he could fuzz out all the undesirable details until the prophet was just a pale, angular face with soft blue eyes and whiskey rolling down slick pink lips.

"Jerry," Hezekiah spoke. Jerry dragged all his attention back to the moment, dropping his gaze down to the brown bottle that the prophet was holding out for him.

Jerry accepted it. "You know, Zeke... I caught myself wondering."

"Wondering, what?" Hezekiah's brow twitched at the nickname.

"What if one day, there is no vision? What if you're sitting here and the Word doesn't come?"

"The Word always comes." A soft *tsk* slipped through Hezekiah's teeth. As he spoke, he dug his fingertips into the base of his skull, rocking his head forward and rolling it around on his neck. "Not that you ever heed what It has to say."

Jerry bit a nodule of gristle on the inside of his cheek and tore it up, washing the wound with a swig of whiskey that left a sting so acute it cleared his nostrils.

He would have loved to be a maggot on the inside of Hezekiah's brain, squirming through all those intricate tunnels and watching the mad visions like a drive-thru theater.

"I hear horns," Hezekiah muttered. He sucked in a hard breath through his nose and raised his head to look at Jerry with his hands still hooked around the back of his neck. "Like Judgment Day. Bodies rising out of the ground..." He hawked and spat between his legs. "The putrid smell of meat."

Jerry offered the prophet another go at the bottle. "What else do you see?"

Hezekiah untangled one hand from His hair and reached out to take the bottle. He grasped it by the neck, and His fingers were bloodless—completely white all the way to the beds of His fingernails.

Hezekiah's mouth fell open and the bottle slipped at the same time. It thudded against the sanctuary carpet and pushed a waterfall of brown liquor out its spout. The sound that staggered out of the prophet's mouth made it sound like He was choking.

"Zeke?" Jerry cast a searching look towards the pews to see if the redhead was going to do anything. Amos' large shadow loomed in the corner of his vision, but his attention was yanked back towards Hezekiah. The prophet's jutting Adam's apple bobbed up and down His narrow throat. His mouth opened wider and wider until Jerry could see every ridge of His white teeth arcing over the darkness of his gullet.

"*Fire in the sky.*" Every word coming out of Hezekiah's mouth sounded as though they were physically painful to utter. "*Thunder like a thousand boots striking the earth...trembling land...great winds stirred by a thousand black wings...!*" Hezekiah clawed at His throat, and His nails left ugly red runs in the white flesh.

Amos' hands came down and grabbed Hezekiah by the shoulders. The redhead pulled the prophet back so that Hezekiah was sitting straight up in His chair, but His corrupted eye was still twitching, shooting from one bloody corner of its socket to the other, bouncing back and forth like it was going to come shooting out of His head. His good eye rolled all the way up and got stuck heavenward, flashing nothing but white.

"Zee!" Amos grabbed Hezekiah's slimy chin, cradling His jaw with one hand while wrapping one arm around the prophet's shoulders to keep Him steady. "Zee, babe, breathe—"

*"The fire in the sky...touches the ground...and the man in its center...burns bright like a wick—the lantern to lead them all—"* Hezekiah's words staggered and halted, and the sound that accompanied them was a long, low moan like some deep-sea leviathan being dragged up from the ocean floor. *"—Burning—God has turned his face away!"*

Hezekiah's body lurched forward, but Amos held Him fast to the seat. The chair shivered and Hezekiah moaned again.

There was blood on his face from where red tears streamed from his corrupted eye. Jerry reached down and picked up the whiskey bottle, nearly cracking his teeth as he brought it to his lips and took a hefty swig of what remained.

"Zee." Amos swiped his thumbs over the prophet's cheeks and pushed sticky strands of Hezekiah's hair away from His eyes. "Are you back with us?"

A dry cough rattled in Hezekiah's throat and He placed His hand against Amos' chest.

"The Tremble is upon us once again." Hezekiah's gaze landed on Jerry as He spoke. "Judgment we cannot outrun." He cleared His throat again. "Jerry, this is beyond spiritual warfare. Everyone in Sweet Providence is going to die."

Jerry stared at Him, unable to comprehend exactly what the prophet was trying to say.

"I don't understand," Jerry admitted.

Hezekiah leaned forward—only a little, since Amos was still mostly in the way. "Everyone," Hezekiah repeated slowly, "is going to die. Every soul in Sweet Providence. They are all meat for Death's mouths—no room for redemption, only repentance."

All of a sudden, Jerry was cold. He rubbed his arms through his blazer, trying not to betray his mounting anxiety while the wheels turned in his head. "That's not something I can put into a sermon," he muttered. He knew it was dumb, but it was all he had.

"I warned you." Hezekiah's words were dark. He looked like He was about to pass out with all that sweat gathering on His brow.

*'Big words coming from a man who looks like a spoiled trout',* was all Jerry could think. Out loud, he said, "I'm not going down without a fight. I don't know a man in that congregation who will, either."

Hezekiah seemed to have lost all interest in him. The prophet turned His head to look up at Amos and gazed up at the redhead through one heavily hooded blue eye.

Amos touched Hezekiah's face tenderly. "I'm going to get you some water," he said.

"Four days," Hezekiah said. "We have four days."

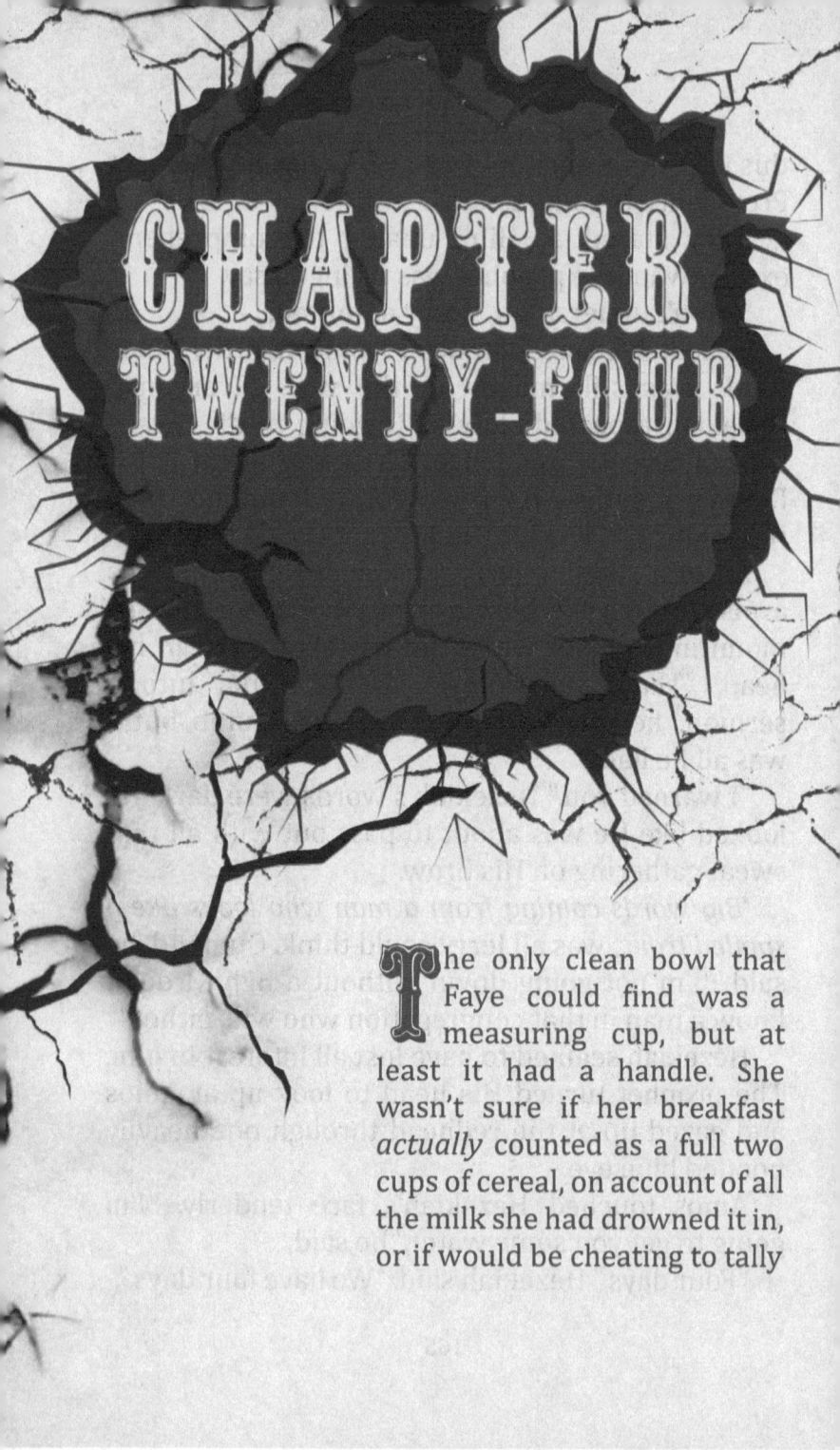

# CHAPTER TWENTY-FOUR

The only clean bowl that Faye could find was a measuring cup, but at least it had a handle. She wasn't sure if her breakfast *actually* counted as a full two cups of cereal, on account of all the milk she had drowned it in, or if would be cheating to tally up her calories based on something closer to a cup-and-a-half. She kept the box of Golden Puffs wedged between her legs, skimming through the panel of nutritional facts on the side while she ate. Ezra's kitchen table was covered in too much *stuff* and she didn't feel like sweeping it off, so the kitchen counter was doubling as her barstool.

According to the box, she had consumed her daily allotment of calories three servings ago. Despite this, she spooned another bite into her mouth. She couldn't help it, she was so *hungry*—more so than she had been in days. Her stomach cramped and gurgled even though she had gone through almost the entire box of cereal. She was already thinking of what she could eat next.

The sound of Ezra's bare feet sticking to the kitchen linoleum brought her head up. Her top lip curled in a way that she couldn't help, and she tried to mask the expression by shoveling another spoonful of Golden Puffs into her mouth.

"Good morning," Ezra said. Up until now, she had never realized exactly how many of his traits were just plumb *irritating.* The way his hair stook up like a rooster's comb with one slide plastered down from being stuck to the pillow; the way he looked at her with that sleepy, vacant expression as if he had any *right* to be tired—he didn't work, he never did anything, really. Except bitch. He was *very* adept at bitching.

"Morning," Faye said. She pressed her tongue against the belly of the spoon and pushed the metal dome up towards the roof of her mouth. Ezra gave her an odd look that she couldn't quite decipher and then walked over to fridge.

"How was the service?" Ezra asked. He pushed his hand through his hair and bent to examine the low refrigerator shelves.

Faye clacked her teeth against the spoon.

"It was good," she said. "*Amazing,* actually. I think Reverend Grievance is exactly what we need. He could preach circles around Jerry any day of the week."

"Oh yeah?" Ezra itched the tip of his nose and then straightened back up. "I don't know. Jerry's preaching isn't all that bad."

Faye pulled the spoon out of her mouth and rolled her eyes. "Riding his dick so hard isn't going to get him to tolerate you any better," she said. "You know that's all he does, right? He only *tolerates* people like us. Grievance *embraces* us. There's a difference—you realize that?"

"Sure." Ezra gave her another strange look. "Did you get any sleep last night? When did you get home?"

"I don't believe that that is any of your *business.*" Faye ate the last bite of her cereal and finished off the sugary milk that remained. "I slept, though. Kind of surprised you stayed in bed as long as you did—since you went to sleep so early."

Ezra paused. His cheeks turned red, and he cleared his throat.

"Looks like I need to go grocery shopping," he muttered. "Want to go with me?"

"Can't," Faye said. "I have to *work.*"

Ezra closed the distance between them and rested his hand on her naked knee.

"Faye," he said, searching her face. "Are you all right?"

"I'm fine," she said. She could *hear* how short she sounded, but she couldn't stop herself. "Why are you looking at me like that?"

"Like what?" He shook his head. "Do you want to at least get some breakfast with me? I can't imagine you're full after just cereal." He tapped the bottom of her measuring cup in emphasis.

The lure of food was enough to make her stomach grumble. As much as she had already eaten, her stomach was giving her signals like she hadn't taken so much as a nibble. It felt twisted tighter than a washrag, to the point where she was almost afraid of the pain that would come if she tried to stand.

"Where do you want to go?" she asked. Her voice faltered a little bit, cracking under her voracious need.

"Anywhere you like," Ezra said. "There's always *Our House.*"

Faye pretended to mull it over for only half a second and then nodded. "Just let me get dressed."

"I don't think they're going to look twice if you walk in wearing pajamas."

"Well, let met at least do something with my hair," she amended.

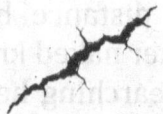

There were vultures in the diner parking lot. Faye counted at least three, and they were all enormous; black-winged with wrinkled red heads that made them look like they had been dipped in blood. Not one of them looked up when Ezra parked near the door, even though his car came dangerously close to bumping into one of them.

All three were standing in a semi-circle, staring at a corner of the alcove that sheltered the diner's entrance. Faye craned her neck to try and get a better look.

"What do you think they've found?" she asked.

"I don't know." Ezra turned off car engine. "Probably a dead cat or something...that's a shame."

"Gross." Faye leaned over a little farther, practically pressing her face against the car window. "You'd think that Mel would have tossed it out back or something, if that was the case."

"She may not have noticed," Ezra said. "We can tell her."

Faye was barely listening to him, anymore. She unbuckled her seatbelt and stepped out of the car, holding onto the door and putting her foot up on the running board to give herself a height boost.

She caught a glimpse of knotted black hair, and at first she thought Ezra was right about the cat. On a second glance, however, she realized that there was no way it could be a cat. It was far too big and sitting too high off the ground.

One of the vultures straightened its posture and spread its enormous black wings. It stood there, perfectly still, for what felt like an eternity before it pulled them back in, like it was wrapping itself up in a cloak, and then shuffled to the side.

Once the bird was out of the way, Faye's stomach launched a rocket full of bile up to her mouth. The smell of dead flesh baking in the late summer heat hit her at the same time as the reveal of raw red hands and a sunken, grey face covered in bristly black hair. One eye was missing, and the full top lip had been ripped away to expose the crooked teeth underneath.

"Oh, fuck, Ezra—fuck, *shit!*" Faye lost her footing and made herself release the car door, rather than risk ripping it off as she fell. She hit the pavement with a thud and a bolt of pain shot up her leg. She hissed and gripped her knee, flicking bits of black asphalt from newly-formed dents while unable to tear her eyes away from the dead man in front of her.

Part of her felt guilty for not recognizing Chris immediately. Although, in her defense, he *was* missing a few pieces.

"Babe, hey! Are you okay?" Ezra gripped his crutch in one hand and held out the other for her. He wasn't looking, and Faye didn't want him to look.

"I busted up my knee," Faye said. "And that's...that's..."

"I know," Ezra said softly. "Don't look at him. Look at me. Take my hand."

"What happened to him, Ezra?" She turned her head long enough to swallow another surge of bile. "I'm going to throw up."

"That's okay," he said. "You can throw up if you need to."

"I don't know how you're staying so fucking calm." She thought that she should feel something—anger, maybe, or even grief. She and Chris had been coworkers for *a lot of years*. They had swapped schedules, colds, and covered one another's asses a multitude of times. And he didn't look like himself. He was like wax. Melting wax. Full of meat. That was all he was, now. Chris West was just meat.

Her stomach spasmed.

"I'm going to tell Mel," Ezra said. "She can call the police. We also need to get you inside. We'll go through the other door."

"I'm not going in there," Faye said. "You can go in if you need to."

Ezra gave her another long, searching look. "I don't want to leave you out here alone," he said.

"I'll be *fine.*" Faye reached behind her and found the car's running board again. She leaned against it and looked up at Ezra—hating the way he was staring at her. Couldn't he just go inside and do what needed to be done, instead of giving her those stupid, needy, *puppy-dog* eyes?

What was wrong with her? Why was she thinking about him that way?

"I'm just worried about you." Ezra pulled back and straightened up, making a face as he re-adjusted his crutch. "I'll be quick. I know Mel has a phone. Then we can get out of here and...go somewhere else."

"Okay." Faye didn't have any fight left. She wrapped her arms around her stomach and curled up, squeezing herself tightly. "I won't go anywhere."

Ezra visibly hesitated, but he finally turned around and walked into the diner. The vultures didn't move. They didn't even acknowledge him. Faye waited until she heard the bell ringing above the restaurant door before lowering herself to her hands and knees and crawling back towards the scene.

The vultures all turned their heads when she approached. There was something *off* about them, but she couldn't decide what it was. She shifted her focus back to Chris, who looked less like a person and more like a crumpled pile of clothes in a donation bin the longer she stared at him.

All the familiar Chris smells were there underneath the hot stink of meat. The cigarette smoke, the mildewed clothes, the dirt on the bottom of his shoes...she wondered if that would have any bearing on the taste.

As soon as that thought slid through her brain, she tried to shake it out. It was revolting, horrifying—and it kept coming back. She continued to crawl, and the vultures just watched. Up close, they were much bigger than they first appeared. Their black feathers held hues of blue and green like puddles of oil, only visible when the sun hit them just right. One of them still had a red string of *Chris-meat* dangling from its bloody beak.

Faye licked her lips. When she finally stopped, she was only inches away from Chris. If she leaned in any closer, they would be able to touch noses— except there wasn't much of his left.

A ragged bit of torn skin stuck up from his cheekbone. Faye's mouth watered—probably from the nausea—and she dragged the back of her hand across her lips. Chris' missing eye had left behind a trail of white slime down his cheek and the vacant hole emitted a foul-smelling heat.

Faye breathed it all in and pushed her face closer, nestling into the space between Chris' tangled black hair and the collar of his oversized denim jacket that reeked of smoke. She slipped her tongue out and pressed it against his skin, not sure what to expect as far as taste. It was mostly bitter, and the smell overpowered all her other senses. She bit

174

down on the raised skin and pulled her head back, just to see what would happen. The skin peeled up too easily, and the exposed flesh underneath was bright red. Faye's heart skipped a beat as the skin came off in one large, satisfying piece, exposing the flesh of her dead coworker's entire cheek.

Hunger stabbed her in the stomach and Faye whined. She lunged towards Chris' body, sinking her teeth into his cheek, tearing off the ivory fat that dribbled oils onto her tongue and shredding the muscle underneath. She clutched Chris' head and gripped his shoulder, gnawing at him like a starved dog. When she finally pulled back, there was a hole in his face that exposed half his teeth and his tongue, and there was so much blood on her chin that she hardly noticed she was crying. Only the sting in her eyes betrayed her.

Faye swung her whole body around and braced herself against the pavement. The vultures closed in around her while making odd, raspy, hissing sounds. One of them in particular, the same one that had spread its wings, was staring her down—and its eyes were human.

*Human,* and the same bright purple as a field of lavender.

Faye screamed. That was the only thing she could think of to drown out the hissing. She crawled away as fast as she could, only just managing to pull herself up to her feet when she found Ezra's car.

She vomited. It was more than just meat. It was cereal, and fur, and tiny bones. It was long strands of black hair and hunks of spongy, undigested fat.

"Faye, Faye!" Ezra's voice broke through everything. The hissing, the screaming, the stomach acid sizzling against the hot pavement. Faye felt hands land on her shoulders and she twisted around, not doubting for a second that she looked as frenzied and wild-eyed as a trapped, feral cat.

Ezra's crutch was on the ground and he was holding her, trying to bring her in as close to his chest as possible. Faye curled up and pressed herself into his arms, burying her face in his shirt and heaving another sob.

"Baby, baby." Ezra stroked her hair. "Shh. It's okay. I'm here."

"I...I ate...oh my g-god..." Faye sniffled and gripped Ezra's shirt even tighter. "I am so, so sorry, Ezra."

"It's okay," Ezra said softly. "It's okay. I know. It's terrible. I know."

He had no reason to be so nice to her. He had no idea what she had just done. He hadn't seen it all, yet. She couldn't let him turn around. Being so close to him was making her hot, and her skin was starting to become unbearably sticky, but the idea of pulling away made her want to vomit all over again. She *could not* let Ezra see what she had done. She couldn't let him look at Chris.

"I want to go home," she whimpered.

"We'll go home," he promised her. "Let's get back into the car, and we will go home."

"Don't look." She clung to him even tighter. "Don't look at him again."

"I won't," Ezra said. "I'm not going to look. I'm going to drive. I'm going to take us home."

Faye nodded. She would have to take him at his word. There was nothing she could do, anyway, if he decided to break it. Faye untangled herself, slowly, and let Ezra pull her up so that she could slide back into the car.

Ezra bent to pick up his crutch and Faye glanced down at the puddle of her own vomit, her heart skipping another beat.

But it was just cereal.

No meat. No hair. No bones.

She didn't want to look at Chris' body again. She didn't want to see if there was a hole in his cheek or if she had hallucinated it all. She wanted to go back to Ezra's house, and she wanted to go to sleep.

He started up the car, and Faye leaned back in her seat. She put her feet up on the dashboard and closed her eyes, keeping them closed for the rest of the drive.

# CHAPTER
# TWENTY-FIVE

**D**awn was the same watery, muddy red as a soaked meat diaper, with clumping purple clouds swirling around like clots. A bucket of swill—that was all Fred could think about. Nasty, big buckets of pig-and-cow stuff being hauled off the butcher room floor. It reminded him of childhood.

The imp probably would have had something to say about it, except it had gone completely silent. Maybe it was dead—he had no way of knowing. Although even if it *was* dead, it was still lodged in the back of his skull. He knew this because he could feel a large heavy *something* sliding around whenever he shook his head or smacked his open palm against the side. Whatever it was made his head hurt like there was a brick sitting on the nape of his neck, and the headache wrapped all the way around to eclipse both eyes.

Fred dragged his boots along the side of the road, kicking up dirt and black bits of asphalt that crumbled away from the rough seam. He had already walked half a mile before realizing he left his car parked in the grass near the dark reverend's tent, and he would be damned if he circled back just for that. He only regretted it because the rising sun, the color of raw egg yolks left to fester on a countertop, dragged up all the worst heat and chased away the shade provided by the few-and-far-between trees.

The imp was gone.

Fred wanted it back.

He didn't know why. He hated that thing. But it was too damn lonely, and he didn't have enough thoughts of his own to fill the void. Fred rubbed his arms as he kept walking, trying to bring himself some sort of comfort by remembering all the words to Johnny Cash's *'I Walk the Line'*. He pinched his nose and itched his nostrils, digging his knuckles against the dry cavities while he stammered out pieces of the lines.

Fred's next step landed wrong, falling into a pothole and twisting his ankle so that it audibly creaked. A white flash of pain overtook his vision, and he staggered towards the center of the road, hopping on his one good foot to avoid putting pressure on the other while he regained his balance.

*"HOO-WEE! Fuck!* City taxes are for shit!" Fred snarled. Once he had steadied himself, he tried to put some pressure back on his injured ankle, but another lightning bolt of pain shot up his leg and he quickly shifted back to the other.

"Fuck." He grabbed his thigh and started hobbling back towards the side of the road. "That's all right, okay? Stop overreacting...it's not that far before we get home. Stupid Fred...stupid pothole...stupid..."

The world switched perspectives so quickly, and so suddenly, that Fred did not have time to register what had happened. One moment, he was looking out towards the horizon at a fuzzy line of dark trees, and then moments later he was staring straight into a too-yellow sun, barely able to squint. For some reason, his eyelids would not shutter, and his corneas were frying.

Fred tried to move, but the most he could manage was making a muscle jump down his right arm. His finger might have twitched, but it was nothing substantial.

He tried to call for help, but his words were smothered by a fountain of blood. At least, that is what it tasted like. The words rose on little foamy bubbles the slid out the sides of his mouth and streamed down the hollows of his cheeks. There was blood in his nose, too. He wanted to cough it out, but he couldn't take a breath.

He had no way of knowing how long he laid there. Finally, Fred's head lolled to the side, cracking every bone in his neck at the same time. The only visual clue he had as to what had happened was a deep red tire tread mark that seemed to run right from his middle, going only a short distance before trailing off into black tracks that careened off the road towards a nearby tree. He couldn't see much further than that—but judging by the fact that the blue station wagon at the end of it all wasn't moving, he doubted that it was in much better shape.

Fred made another attempt at taking a deep breath, but his lungs felt like they were full of holes.

A shadow stretched across the pavement—the figure of a tall man in a wide-brimmed black hat. Fred tried desperately to lift his head off the road and get a better look, but he couldn't manage it at all, not even an inch.

The shadow shrank as it moved across the asphalt, seemingly creeping closer. Something black finally danced into Fred's peripheral vision, and then he saw that it wasn't a person at all. It was just a vulture. It stared at him with eyes that were far too human, lavender and heavily lidded, making the bird itself look like it was from a cartoon.

Fred grimaced. He wished he could raise his arm just to shoo the damn thing away.

*'Get out of hear, dumb bird,'* he thought. *'I'm not your roadkill breakfast.'*

Even as the words passed through his brain, another vulture landed close to the first, and then another. More shadows appeared as the sky began to fill with enormous black birds, circling the atmosphere above his head in a way that, from his position, resembled a cyclone.

The vulture that appeared first spread its large, cobalt wings. For a moment, it stood in the growing sunlight, its iridescent black feathers drenched in hues of flaming orange and blood red.

After what felt like an eternity, the bird settled back down and draped its wing over Fred's face. A small mercy, he supposed, if a somewhat unnecessary one.

Because aside from the yanking and pulling, he couldn't really feel anything at all.

# CHAPTER TWENTY-SIX

There were blue police lights on Deer Head, which was what Isabel supposed she deserved for trying to avoid traffic by taking a back road. There wasn't really a good way to turn around, either. She was trapped behind her steering wheel until further notice.

What a crappy way to spend a Friday. All she wanted was to get her hair done.

Several police cars blocked off her view from the scene, but there were black vultures scattered on both sides of the narrow road. Some of them had

shreds of red meat dangling from their beaks, while some seemed to be looking straight at *her*, like she was next.

It felt like an eternity before a police officer knocked on her window. Isabel let out a pre-emptively grateful sigh and cranked the window down so that the office could stick his head in.

Now that he was up close, she recognized him as Dale Runner, a regular Sunday attendee.

"Sorry to hold you up like this, Sister Calhoun." Officer Dale sounded genuinely apologetic.

"It's all right." Isabel drummed her fingernails on the steering wheel, fighting the urge to try and get a better peek. "What happened?"

"Really awful accident," Officer Dale muttered. "Don't want to get too into detail but there's a reason we tried to block it all off. Really nasty scene, ma'am." He pushed up the brim of his hat and swept his hand underneath it. "Is Pastor Calhoun able to come get you?"

"He is at the church," Isabel said. "Besides, he would be just as stuck." She looked around. "What are the chances of me getting out of here, soon?"

"I'll have one of my boys move us out of the way so you can turn around," Officer Dale said. "Try not to look too hard though, Sister Calhoun, if you *do* see anything. Like I said, it's really nasty—"

She did not even catch the remainder of what he said. A flash of familiar copper hair arrested her attention and Isabel turned her head, looking over to see Jonah seated halfway in the backseat of a police car with a blanket wrapped around his shoulders. She caught herself staring, but only because she wasn't sure if it *was* him at first. He looked like he had taken a bucket of sand to the face. His already-crooked nose was busted and bloody, and his right eye was so black that it had swollen shut.

"Sister Calhoun?" Officer Dale asked.

"Is that Jonah Sweet?" Isabel shot back. "What is going on here?"

Officer Dale sighed. "Can't rightly tell you for sure, ma'am, 'cause we don't know. We think his car spun out of control and..."

Isabel didn't even give him the chance to finish. She had already unbuckled and was opening up her car door. The officer backed up to give her room and she walked right past him, forcing herself not to run all the way up to where Jonah was sitting.

The minute she stopped to take a breath, she inhaled the scent of sharp, metallic scent of blood on hot, spoiled meat. Isabel gagged and threw her hand over her mouth to try and minimize the effect.

"Jonah?" she asked. He looked up as soon as he heard his name.

"Izzy." He reached up with one covered hand and rubbed the corner of his blanket against his face. "Oh, my God, Isabel. Everything is so bad."

"Did you lose control of your car?" She knelt down beside him, suddenly not caring at all about her pantyhose or how the asphalt pierced right through them and dug into her knees.

"Something was off," Jonah's throat sounded tight. "I think a tie rod broke. I couldn't steer, then I couldn't brake. I don't know. It all happened so fast..." He cracked his swollen lid. The eye underneath was ghastly white in contrast to the surrounding purple flesh. "I think Joel is dead."

"Joel...?" Isabel tried to feel something at the thought, but she could barely bring herself to picture Hezekiah's bohemian lover, much less mourn them. Jonah was her primary concern, and at least he was alive. She could do something about *that*.

"They haven't told me for sure, but I know it," Jonah leaned forward just a little. "I *know* that Presley is dead."

Presley.... "Fred Presley?" Isabel asked. Jonah responded with a nod. There was another name that wouldn't be missed and, if anything, now her Sundays would be a little quieter.

She didn't say that, of course. She just took Jonah's hands in hers.

Only half a second later she realized how it might look. Isabel pressed her hand against the back of Jonah's head and yanked it down.

"I'm praying for you," she hissed. Jonah stared at her, bewildered, but nodded again.

"We need to get you to a doctor," Isabel whispered.

"I can't," Jonah said. "Joel is dead. I need to find Hezekiah and Amos, and..."

"It's Babylon Prayer day. You can afford to take an hour and make sure nothing is broken."

Jonah whimpered. Isabel could not stop the full-body shiver of revulsion that was her knee-jerk reaction to such a pathetic sound.

"Stop that!" Isabel snapped, perhaps a little harsher than was warranted. "God, that smell is killing me. I'll tell Dale that I'm driving you home."

Jonah rubbed the blanket against his face again. "I'm going to puke," he said. "I already did once, but I think I'm going to do it again."

"Okay," Isabel said. "Just do it before you get into the car."

# CHAPTER TWENTY-SEVEN

**T**he howl that came tearing out of Hezekiah's mouth at the news of Joel's death was beyond animalistic. It was deeper, heavier, more like wind whipping down a train tunnel, pain amplified by emptiness.

Jerry had never heard the prophet scream like that. He didn't know that Hezekiah had the capacity for so much emotion.

Amos was shaking and looked ready to vomit, but he didn't stray from Hezekiah's side. He kept one

arm out, ready to catch the prophet, who looked like He was about to crumple.

Officer Dale Runner looked as uncomfortable as Jerry had ever seen him. Poor man probably drew the short straw when they were passing around lots to see who was going to tell the Prophet that His lover was dead.

"Real sorry about that, Hezekiah," Jerry said in an attempt to smother the emotional burn pile. "Joel was a good kid." Jerry had really only met them once, and all he remembered was that they wore earrings made out of trash and seemed allergic to shoes.

Hezekiah kept His hand planted firmly on His chest. It moved up and down with each heaving breath, and His whole body quivered.

"Where is Jonah?" He asked. His voice croaked as He spoke. Officer Dale threw a look over at Jerry and then cleared his throat.

"Well, um," he said, "Sister Calhoun was stopped by the accident and offered to take Brother Sweet to a doctor."

Amos looked up. His eyes found Jerry, too, but he clearly did not share the officer's embarrassment.

There was something else on his face, and Jerry wasn't keen on reading into it too deeply.

"So, Isabel's out of town?" Jerry took a deep breath. "Wish she had called me."

"She clearly had *better* things to do, Jerry," Hezekiah snarled.

"Where is Joel now?" Amos asked, turning back to the officer. He was clearly trying his best to keep himself in one piece, but it wasn't easy judging from the white-knuckled grip he had on Hezekiah's arm.

"We sent them down to the funeral home," Officer Dale said. "They'll need someone down there to identify the body and then, well…I am not sure of the procedure of these things when there isn't any blood family involved." The officer shrugged weakly and then turned his attention back to Jerry. "There is something else I've got to ask you about, preacher."

"What is it?" Jerry asked, stepping through the opening in the conversation where he could clearly take charge.

"Fred Presley doesn't—*didn't*—have any family either," he said. "We sent him down to the funeral home as well, but there's no one we can reach out to for the arrangements. I assume—well—is the church going to be able to take care of that?"

Jerry sucked in a deep breath and bit the inside of his cheek. Fred Presley had been a loyal member of the congregation, even if he had also been the least liked. Maybe Jerry didn't *owe* him anything, but it would no doubt be frowned upon by the rest of the congregation if their pastor didn't at least try to make sure the poor guy had a proper burial.

Although just thinking about the cost—a casket, flowers, a plot, a headstone—was making his head spin. The funeral home would cut them a deal, he was sure, but it would mean dipping into the church coffers which required deacon approval. Isabel usually handled that, and she was out making sure some two-buck fag was getting his boo-boos examined.

Another deep breath and Jerry tweaked his own nose to bring himself back to the moment.

"I'm sure that we can do something for him," Jerry said. "Won't be anything fancy, but we can take up an offering. I'll go down and talk to the funeral home to see what we can arrange." He looked at Hezekiah, uncertain of whether he should even ask what was on his mind. "And do you...?"

"We already have a family plot," Hezekiah choked. "You don't need to be concerned about any of us, Jerry." The prophet grabbed Amos' hand and squeezed it in His own. "It's the beginning of the end," Hezekiah said. "I guess God wanted to spare Joel the agony of watching everything go up in flames."

*"For the Lord himself will descend from heaven with a cry of command, with the voice of an archangel, and with the sound of the trumpet of God. And the dead in Christ will rise first."* Jerry quoted the tired verse, the one given at every funeral.

Hezekiah shot him a dire look.

"Then I'll see them again," Hezekiah spat. "Only four more sleeps until our Final Day."

# CHAPTER TWENTY-EIGHT

When Ezra walked through his front door, the first thing he did was hang up his keys and kick his flip-flops towards the wall. The second thing he did was shuffle into the kitchen to make some tea, keeping an eye on Faye as he did so.

She had been quiet for the entire ride home. Now that they were back, she had found a seat at the kitchen table and was just sitting there with her arms resting against the surface and her face buried in her arms. Her sweaty gold curls fell in every direction, completely concealing her head under one giant puff.

Ezra puttered around the kitchen, opening and closing cabinets to try and occupy his hands while water boiled in the kettle. Ideally, he would make something for them to eat—but after what they had just seen, he doubted either of them had much of an appetite.

He refilled Winston's bowl and scratched his dog's soft golden ears.

Finally, the kettle whistled. Ezra never poured anything so quickly in his life.

Faye didn't look up until he set a mug of hot tea in front of her. As soon as the ceramic bottom hit the wooden table she peeked over her folded arms, large brown eyes so dilated they looked black.

"Thank you," Faye muttered. She rested her pointed chin on the back of her wrist and stared at the steaming mug. Ezra nodded and sat down beside her, cradling his own mug in his hands and savoring the warmth.

"You should drink it, before it gets cold," he urged gently. Faye huffed, blowing a stray curl off her nose.

"I think I'll throw up if I try," she said. Ezra shook his head.

"It's mint, it will settle your stomach," he said. He wanted to say something else, like '*try not to think about it*', but if she was *already* trying to forget about *it*, then he didn't want to bring it back to her mind.

"I think I need to go lay down," Faye said. She snatched a curl from mid-air and dragged it around her cheek. She stuck the end in her mouth and chewed on it, looking up at him again with those enormous eyes made of sweet brown sugar toffee. "Will you go with me?"

Ezra gave her a long look and sipped his tea. Lying beside Faye was likely one of his only options for suppressing *the horrors* and the mental image of Chris' dead, skeletal, dried-up face. They hadn't slept together in years, not even platonically, since their break-up. It was more for his sake—his feelings were too easily tangled and he wasn't very good at separating degrees of intimacy. But now, they were both unsettled and terrified, and Faye was asking for him directly.

Surely, his messy, sticky feelings could be pushed down long enough to be a decent friend. Or at least, a decent person who was still in love with Faye Warren, and wanted to comfort her when she asked.

"Sure," he finally said. "I'll come with you. I'm taking my tea—do you want yours?"

Faye shook her head. Ezra savored another sip of tea before standing and walking towards his bedroom. Winston stood at the same time and followed him while Faye moved past, always having to be a few steps ahead. She practically dove into Ezra's bed, grabbing his pillow and wrapping her arms around it. Winston jumped onto the bed as well, but Ezra shooed him off. It was nowhere big enough for the three of them.

"Feel better?" Ezra asked. Faye nodded and buried her face in his pillow, huffing.

"This is much better," she said. "I don't feel like I'm going to be sick anymore."

"Well, that's good," Ezra said. He took one more sip of his tea and then set the cup down on his bedside table. "Can I get you anything? I can turn on the TV if you would like…?"

Faye shook her head. She inch-wormed her way across the bed and curled up against Ezra's side, tucking her face against his ribs and wrapping her legs around his. Ezra froze for half a second before placing his arm around her shoulders, drawing her in close and hesitating only a little before dropping a kiss onto her hair.

"It's going to be okay," he whispered.

"I wish I believed that," Faye whispered back. "I wish I knew what happened to Chris."

"Me too," Ezra said. "I guess he was pretty sick."

"Do you think that did it?" Faye shivered. "That's so fucked."

"Yeah," Ezra agreed. "It's really sad. He sounded really bad last night..." he shut his mouth as soon as he realized what he was saying. Faye lifted her head and looked up at him, furrowing her brow.

"Last night?" she asked. "I thought you went to bed early?"

Ezra's heart rate doubled almost immediately. "I did," he said. "But then the phone rang, and..."

"And...?" Faye sat up.

"Mabel Calhoun needed my help," Ezra's mouth felt dry, suddenly, but his tea was too far away to reach without contorting. "She blew and tire, and I went to pick her up. We waited it out at the diner, no big deal."

"Oh, I see," Faye snorted. "So, you were too busy to give *me* a ride, but not too busy to go somewhere with *Mabel?*"

"What is your problem with her?" Ezra challenged.

"Nothing," Faye said. "I don't have a problem with *her.* Other than the fact that she has the personality of a towel. But *you* said that your 'mobility wasn't too good', and then you go out and run around with Mabel Calhoun all night? Jesus!" She turned away, as if she was too disgusted to even continue. Faye threw her legs off the side of the bed and Ezra reached out for her.

"Come on, Faye," he said. "It isn't anything like that, I promise. Mabel had an emergency; I was the first person she called who picked up."

"And she couldn't have called a taxi?" Faye rolled her eyes. "That's some *top-tier* damsel-in-distress bullshit, let me tell you."

"Oh, lay off it!" Ezra snapped. He regretted his tone almost immediately, but he didn't back down. "You're mad that I didn't go with you, I get that, but—"

"Actually, I am mad that you lied to me," Faye said. "You could have just said *'fuck off, Faye, I don't feel like going with you tonight.'*"

"Oh, come on," Ezra said. "That's not something I would ever say to you. I really was in pain, and I slept for a little while. The phone rang, I answered. What was I supposed to do? Say *'no'*?"

Faye shook her head and waved her hand dismissively. "I'm not doing this," she said. "I'm not going to beat this into the ground with you."

"Where are you going?" Ezra's heart dropped a whole floor inside his chest. He hated, hated, *hated* arguing with Faye—but they both jumped into it so easily.

"It's still Revival," Faye said. "There's a service tonight. I'm going to go."

"Okay," Ezra said. "But that's tonight. You should rest a little bit more beforehand. I'll leave you alone, I'll go to the couch."

"Don't bother," Faye said. "I need to get out of this house anyway."

"Where are you going to go?" Ezra asked. "I mean, I know you can go anywhere you want, I just..."

"I don't know yet," Faye said. "I just need to clear my head. Don't worry, though," she tossed her head and shot him a sarcastic look. "I won't call you if I need anything."

"For the love of God, Faye...!"

She didn't respond to him. Faye slipped out of the room and Winston stood up to follow her. Ezra leaned over the side of the bed and grabbed his dog's collar to keep him back.

The sound of Faye's footsteps paused for only a few seconds, then picked back up right before the front door slammed shut.

# CHAPTER
## TWENTY-NINE

**W**ithin a matter of hours, the sky had turned putrid, swampy green. Dark grey clouds overburdened with impending rain crowded each other like dumplings in a pot. Jerry's favorite radio station kept fading in and out of static to the point where he just switched it off to avoid punching the dashboard in frustration. *'Some storm brewing. I doubt they'll be having a tent revival in the rain.'*

One could never be sure. Fringe zealots were unpredictable. Jerry pulled into the grass near the big white tent where the only other car in sight was Presley's beat-up old Crown Vic.

Just the sight of that thing was like looking at Fred's corpse itself. Jerry shivered and pulled down his visor, like that would somehow block his vision enough for him to collect his bearings.

The wind was already picking up by the time he got out of the car. Not enough to bend the grass, but enough to make it sway around his boots. The sides of the tent wobbled, as if one good gust would be enough to pluck the stakes right out of the ground and send the whole thing flying. Jerry fidgeted by straightening his tie and started walking towards the front entrance, scratching between his legs as hard as possible to try and calm down the unbearable itching before coming face-to-face with another human being.

There was no guarantee that the reverend *would* be there, he supposed. It was just the only place he knew to look.

"Hello?" Jerry called out as he approached the tent. No one answered, so he poked his head inside and glanced around. Inside the tent had an odd smell—he had no way to describe it other than *formaldehyde,* and even then, he wasn't sure why *that* in particular.

"Jeremiah Donald Calhoun," a voice interrupted his thoughts, and Jeremiah nearly jumped out of his skin. "I've been waiting a long time."

There was no one inside the tent. A long shadow fell in front of Jerry, outstretching his own by a mile, and he slowly turned his head to glance over his shoulder.

The smell of formaldehyde was even stronger, mixed with a bouquet of florals that smelled like the peace lily and baby's breath arrangements that arrived in droves at funerals.

"Good afternoon," Jerry said, trying to stay polite despite the way his pulse was racing in his throat. He took another two steps forward just so he could rotate properly, and that was when he saw the reverend standing in the tent entrance.

It was like staring death in the face. There was no other way to describe it. Grey liver-spotted skin, shriveled purple lips, and eyes sunken so deep that their sockets appeared hollow.

Jerry swallowed hard. "Reverend Grievance?" He asked, putting on his best Christmas Eve Service smile, the one he wore to dazzle the relatives of special-occasion-only Christians. "I've heard a lot about you."

The reverend gave a long, thin-lipped smile, but he didn't say a word.

Jerry tried again. "I'm dreadfully sorry to come in unannounced," he said. "I'm sure you must have heard that there's been an accident." He looked around, searching for anything his eyes could linger on other than the creepy figure.

"The one involving Fred Presley, and Joel Harding?" The reverend shook his head. "I know about it. I was there." He brought his hands in front of him and placed his fingertips together. His fingers were so long and crooked that they didn't look real. "Tragic. And just down the road from us, too. Let me tell you, Fred was certainly on fire for the Lord. He brought quite the spark to our humble Revival services."

"Yes, well," Jerry fought against rolling his eyes. "Fred was something, I'll say that. 'Course, you'll probably be shocked to hear he had no family." His words became more clipped as Jerry set his teeth on edge. He wasn't sure if it was because he was nervous, or because he was sweating, but the itching was becoming unbearable. It took every ounce of his self-control not to claw at the front of his slacks.

"He had his church family," the reverend said.

Jerry's patience was drying up faster than a puddle of spilled gasoline in June. The longer he looked at the reverend, the more he realized that something was most definitely not right. The reverend's mouth had started to droop farther and farther down until the corners were piling up right by his chin. His large, heavily lidded eyes were a nearly comical exaggeration of sympathy, emphasized by his thin, knit brows.

"Yes," that damn itching. Jerry grabbed his waistband and tried to hike it up discreetly, hoping the moving fabric would alleviate some of his problem. "Fred had us, and we're all brothers and sisters in Christ, but he had no *blood* family. And you said that he was coming here the last few days of his life, wasn't he?"

"He was," the reverend said. "He gave his testimony. It was very powerful."

"Oh, yes," Jerry said. "Powerful indeed. It sounds like Fred touched you, particularly. And look, I'm not here to take away any man's uhm..." he hiked up his waistband again. "...dammit. Forgive me, it's hard to talk about um, Fred."

The reverend reached out and touched Jerry's shoulder. His touch was ice cold. Even through the layers of Jerry's blazer and dress shirt, he felt the chill down to the bone.

"Say what is on your mind," the reverend told him.

"I..." it was hard for Jerry to concentrate with the chill spreading downward. It moved fast and hit his belly first, but it didn't stop there. It spread soothing numbness like a menthol muscle rub until the itching was completely gone. "Well, I was just wondering if *you* would like to be the one to give his sermon."

The reverend held his gaze. Those large lavender eyes were so mournful. Grief punched Jerry in the gut and he nearly burst into tears on the spot.

What the hell was wrong with him?

204

"If I do that," the reverend said, "it would only be right if I covered the funeral as well."

"Oh, I wouldn't insist," Jerry straightened.

"Oh, but I would," the reverend pulled his hand back and rested it against his chest. "Eulogies are something of a specialty of mine."

"Well," Jerry felt the relief in his own smile. "I wouldn't take that from you, then. And I do appreciate it—I mean I *really do* appreciate it. Fred deserves to be honored and his passing was just senselessly tragic."

"I wholly agree," the reverend said. He looked Jerry up and down. "You will have your hands full without Fred, I reckon."

"Will I?" Jerry was already turning to leave.

"Joel Harding was also a member of your congregation, weren't they?"

"Ah," Jerry made a face. "I reckon I will have to say a few words."

"I truly believe that as pastors, we have the most difficult jobs of all. We bear the weight of all their sins, and all their grief."

"Like Jesus on the cross," Jerry snorted.

"Something like that," the reverend mused. "It makes you wonder, too. Who will be delivering your eulogy, when you die?"

Jerry swiped at the corners of his mouth. It wasn't exactly a topic he was keen to dwell on. "Well, I admit, I've never given it much thought," he said. "Maybe you will, if you're still around."

The reverend's cavernous frown turned upward, only slightly. A movement like a stop-motion clay figurine.

# CHAPTER THIRTY

On any other stormy day, Mabel would have been happy to curl up with a book and get lost in its pages. However, despite her best attempts, she had not progressed past her bookmark and felt like she was reading the same paragraph over and over.

There was no rain yet, but the sky had been hideous since she returned with her mother's car. Even so, the heavy cloud cover did not offer any relief from the heat, it just made it a touch more bearable to sit out on the porch.

Mabel gave up. She shut her book and set it down on the glass-top wicker table beside the wooden porch swing. The rusty chains groaned in protest as she stretched out one leg and pressed her toes against the side of the house to rock herself backwards.

It was hard not to feel like a failure. All that time spent getting straight A's, evangelizing instead of making friends, volunteering when she could have been working a real job, setting her sights on boys who turned around and told her that they were 'focusing on their relationship with Christ'. In the past three years she had attended multiple weddings held at the church, but she was never even a bridesmaid. Being the pastor's daughter didn't get her anything, except scrutiny.

She had to wonder if it was too late—if there was nothing else she could do to pop her life back onto the tracks. She had worn out her welcome within the walls of her own home, but what else was there? She could rent a townhome, get a job at a bookstore, maybe adopt a cat. Her dad always said that women who lived alone with cats turned into sad, ugly spinsters who were doomed to babysit the children they could have parented.

She wondered how true that was.

A car rolled into view and Mabel stretched out her foot again to stop the swing. She leaned over to get a better look, smiling when she recognized the familiar dark burgundy.

Ezra Buchanan rolled down his window and waved at her. Mabel waved back and dismounted the swing, walking barefoot down the hot walkway to say 'hello'.

"Hey, Mabel," Ezra said. Mabel smiled and bent to rest her arms against the car windowsill.

"Hey, Ezra," she greeted in return. "What are you doing out and about?"

"I was looking for Faye," Ezra glanced down the street. "She kind of ran off. I haven't been able to find her, though."

"Oh," Mabel said. "That's a shame." She pursed her lips. "I can help you look, if you want the company."

"Are you sure? I don't want to mess up your plans."

"I don't have any plans," Mabel huffed dramatically. "Unless you count *Anna Karenina*. But I'll put down Tolstoy for you."

"That's very generous," Ezra let out a light laugh. "Okay, hop in."

"Well, let me get my shoes." Mabel patted the windowsill. "Don't go anywhere, I'll be right back."

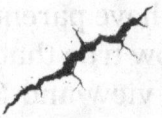

After over an hour of driving around with nothing to show for it, Ezra finally had to stop for gas. Mabel took the opportunity to stretch her legs and grab them some Cokes and honeybuns. She tossed one into Ezra's lap as soon as he sat back down, unable to stop herself from giggling at the look on his face when a plastic-wrapped pastry came hurling at him.

"Sorry," Mabel said. "I thought you could use a snack."

"Oh, I see. Well, thank you." Ezra broke open the packaging and peeled it away so he could take a bite. "I will be honest—I'm at the point where I am about to give up."

"You know Faye," Mabel said. "She'll turn up when she's ready. She didn't give you anything about where she was going to be?"

"Well," Ezra rubbed the back of his neck. "I know she's going to be at that tent revival tonight. But…"

"But…?" Mabel tilted her head.

"I don't know," Ezra said. "Something about that whole thing is off. I wish I could explain it better."

"Well, if you don't want to go alone, I could go with you," Mabel said. "Maybe it won't be so bad if you have someone you can escape with."

"Maybe," Ezra sounded a bit doubtful. "It's really strange. I guess it's just not what I'm used to."

"I bet," Mabel took another swig of her Coke. "But I don't mind going."

Ezra nodded and took another bite of his honeybun. Mabel watched him from the corner of her eye, tapping her teeth against the glass rim of her bottle.

It was getting easier for her to see Ezra as a boy. She barely remembered what he looked like before he started sprouting chin hair and sideburns, other than the fact that he had a somewhat round face, and his hair used to be a lot longer. Now his face had hollowed out a bit more and his hair was well above his ears. There were a thousand questions on the tip of her tongue that she was almost desperate to ask. *'What else is different?' 'Have you had any surgeries?' 'Once you're done with everything...are you going to be able to start a family with a woman?'*

She held them back, smothering them with the Coke fizz gathering on her tongue. When she finally pulled her mouth from the bottle, Ezra looked over at her, raising one eyebrow like he could sense the barrage of unasked questions that was making her whole body tremble.

"You okay?" he asked. Mabel nodded. She started to say something, and then choked on her own words. Nothing was going to come out the way she wanted it to, and the last thing she wanted to do was offend him. But she didn't want to just sit there

211

staring at him, wide-eyed with her mouth gaping open. He was going to think she was insane.

To smother the awkwardness, Mabel leaned in and brushed her lips over Ezra's cheek. He froze, his entire face turning the same color as a can of cranberry sauce.

Mabel smiled. She couldn't help it.

"You are so cute," she giggled.

"Sorry," he ducked his head. "I just wasn't expecting that."

"I hope I didn't upset you," she told him.

"No, no," he said quickly. "Not at all." He turned back to her and leaned over the center seat. He pecked her cheek in return and then retreated back to his side, clearing his throat and taking a heavy swig of his soda before turning the car back on.

"So," she teased him, "are we going to church?"

"I guess so," Ezra said. If he was trying to hide his bashful smile, he was doing a bad job. "Do I get another kiss, if we survive it?"

"I will think about it," Mabel said, "but I think your chances are very good."

# CHAPTER THIRTY-ONE

The grim reverend's congregation was gathered outside of the revival tent. The crowd had doubled in size from the night before, to the point where there were bodies spilling out into the street. Faye skirted along the edge until she found an opening and then started elbowing her way through, not caring about the dirty looks that were being shot her way.

Reverend Grievance stood at the entrance of the tent with the crowd forming a semi-circle in front of him. They were packed in tightly, shoulder-to-shoulder with one another to cram as many seeking faces and reaching hands into his space as possible. The reverend's hands were raised with his palms turned towards Heaven, where the sky was such a dark shade of green that it was almost pitch-black.

Faye froze only about three feet away from the reverend. Anywhere else, a crowd that size would have made her hot-foot it out of there as quickly as possible. But here and now, things were different. These people were her family—*Grievance* was her family.

This was the only place where she was truly wanted. *Welcomed.*

Grievance turned his face towards her and beckoned with one outstretched hand. Faye inched her way closer until she was within touching distance. While every eye in the crowd was burning holes into the back of her head.

"Faye," Reverend Grievance reached out and touched the sides of her face. "It is time. Can you feel the tremble?"

Faye stared up into those soft lavender eyes and shook her head. "I can't feel anything, reverend," she told him. Her hands trembled as she reached up and set her fingers against the back of his. His touch was almost unbearably warm.

"Reach deeper," Grievance said. "You can feel it if you pay attention."

Faye had no idea what he was talking about, but she closed her eyes regardless, trying to feel what he described. He stroked her cheekbones with his thumbs, cradling her head like she was something precious. With each caress, Faye slipped farther into herself, allowing her restless spirit to be soothed. She drew in a deep breath through her mouth and circulated it out through her nose. She repeated that three times, the third breath leaving her shoulders sagging and her head lolling, easily manipulated by the reverend's fingers.

Then, she felt the tremble.

It began as a quiver underneath her feet. It penetrated her soles and made her arches tingle and itch. It spread up her ankles and to her calves, drawing her muscles taut and making them jump until her knees jerked. Her heart started racing, pumping blood at a dizzying speed. She felt like she was falling, even though she was still rooted to the same spot, being held oh-so-tenderly in the reverend's hands. The entire world spun through the darkness behind her eyelids, where spots of light began to appear and explode like fireworks.

"I feel it," Faye whispered, craving the approval she knew was waiting on the other side.

"Bless the Lord," Grievance gripped her head even tighter. "That tremble is within the earth. This sinner's ground will split in twain and swallow the dens of iniquity and degradation. Then all will be well, all will be well within your souls."

Faye opened her eyes and looked up at the reverend. He wasn't gazing down at her, as she expected, he was addressing the crowd while clutching her tight. He had her head pulled down so that her forehead was close to touching his chest.

Faye twisted free from his grasp and the reverend finally looked at her again. She could still feel the tremble like the grit side of a nail file running across every frayed nerve in her fingers and toes. It drilled deep into her jawbone until her *teeth* itched.

"What do you mean, the ground will split?" she asked.

"I mean it exactly as it sounds," the reverend said. "Everything must sink. Buried, to build anew."

An ear-splitting *boom* followed by a long, loud roar cut off the reverend's sermon at its crescendo. The ground shifted and shook, swaying like it had been suddenly cut loose from the end of a taut string. Members of the congregation dropped to their knees in clumps, some landing on their faces, and every one of them screaming at the tops of their throats. They begged for forgiveness, some raising their hands towards the sky and speaking in tongues. Tears streamed down their flushed faces as they thrashed and howled, rolling around in the dirt as if they were possessed. The ground continued to shake, and another *boom* gave birth to a wide, dark split right underneath Faye's feet.

Faye did everything she could to remain upright. She hopped back and stumbled, swinging around on one leg to hop to the next patch of seemingly stable ground.

"And the Lord will bring a great reckoning!" Reverend Grievance stretched his hands even higher. "Where giants shall walk the earth!"

Dead air stirred into howling wind, picking up as suddenly as if it had been blown from a divine mouth.

Once Faye regained her balance, she did not lose her momentum. She ran into the crowd, skirting the bodies that had crumpled to the ground and not hesitating to throw herself into the ones who hadn't. No one fought her. Every time her hands came into contact with someone's shoulders or ribs, they staggered and fell back. The ground did most of the work. It buckled and widened the existing crack, prying the earth apart from underneath the crust.

There were shrieks and howls like the screams of the damned. Faye had no way of telling whether they came from above the split, or underneath.

It wasn't far to the edge of the road. She kept running, even though there was no destination in mind. A burgundy car pulled up just as she hit the asphalt and she threw her hands out in front of her, as if that alone would be enough to stop an oncoming vehicle.

The car screeched to a halt. Once it was no longer in motion, she recognized it immediately as Ezra's. She ran over to the passenger side window and started banging on it with her fist.

"Ezra!" She was already screaming. "Ezra, open the door!"

The passenger side window rolled down, and the first thing she saw was Mabel Calhoun's freckled face. Faye couldn't stop the disgusted look that crossed her face.

"Ezra," Faye stuck her head through the window, looking right past Mabel like she didn't exist. "We need to get out of here!" She opened the passenger door and nudged Mabel—not gently—in the shoulder. "Scoot over, chickadee."

Mabel slid over until she was wedged into the center front seat. Faye grabbed the door and pulled it shut, glancing out the window while she cranked it back up.

"What is going on?" Ezra asked, employing that hopeless lack of observation Faye was usually fond of, but not in this moment.

"The world is ending," Faye said flatly. "At the very least, you're speeding through an earthquake. I need you to get somewhere safe."

"Where are we going to go?" Ezra asked.

"My house," Mabel said. "It's closer than yours."

"Like hell," Faye snapped.

"We need to slow down, if not stop altogether, and wait this out," Mabel shot back. "You're not asking Ezra to drive across town through an earthquake."

"We won't stay long," Ezra said, maybe his own version of trying to diffuse the tension that was building in the car faster than the pressure outside.

218

"We will wait for this to subside and then we will figure out what to do. Do you think that the congregation—?"

Before he could get anything else out, Faye slammed her hand on the dashboard. The impact was like a gunshot going off.

"Right now, Grievance's congregation is out there losing its damn mind," she said. "I don't want to go back there, I want you to *step on it.*"

Thankfully, Ezra did not need to be told a third time. He sped off down the road while Faye kept her eyes on the rearview mirror, dreading the sight of anyone trying to follow them.

But no one did.

# CHAPTER
# THIRTY-TWO

As soon as Ezra pulled into Mabel's driveway, she slid over Faye's lap and grabbed hold of the passenger door. She jumped out before the car engine even stopped rumbling, trying to keep steady while darting up the porch steps and making sure the door was unlocked so that Faye and Ezra could run in. The wind knocked the porch swing back and forth so violently that the chains scraped against the white posts. A heady gust nearly ripped the storm door off its hinges, bending it so far back that it made a loud *snap.*

Mabel glanced over her shoulder and gestured for them to follow her before stepping further into the house. Inside, without the buffeting wind to drown out every other sound, she heard the notes of an old Gospel song drifting through the kitchen.

As if it was being pulled on a line, Mabel's head snapped in the direction of her father's room. Her mouth went dry and she started walking towards the kitchen, unsure of how she was going to explain this situation. There was evidence of the earthquake on the walls with tilted pictures and fallen candles, but between leaving the car and hearing the radio, the tremors had nearly completely subsided.

She didn't look behind her to see if Faye and Ezra were in the house, she could only assume they were. She *hoped* that Ezra would not speed off and drive away without her, but the longer she was home, the sillier she was starting to feel. Earthquakes were frightening, but it was over now, and Faye had likely been spooked by what was a fairly typical revival. She just hadn't been to church in so long that she had no idea of what it looked like when people were possessed by the Holy Spirit. That was what revivals were *for.*

Mabel reached her father's door and paused to knock. At first, there was no response, but the radio got a little louder. She knocked again.

"Daddy?" she pressed her face close to the wood. "Are you okay?"

There was a long pause, and then the doorknob turned.

The door came open just a fraction and her father appeared in the dark slit. For half a second, Mabel didn't recognize him. His face was haggard and his thin, dark hair stuck out in all directions. He looked like he had been sleeping, but when he raised his hand, his fingers were covered in dark, glossy brown slime.

"I hoped you were your mother," he said. His voice sounded like he had been gargling glass.

"What happened to you?" Mabel started to reach out, then drew back her hand. "Are you alright? Do I need to call someone-?"

Jerry glanced down at his own fingers and flipped his hand over front and back, as if he was seeing the entire appendage for the first time. "It's really funny," he said. "I prayed for healing. But you know, sometimes you ask God for something, and he just says *no*." He let out a dry, rattling cough and then shot a look past Mabel's shoulder. "Who did you bring here?"

"It's Ezra Buchanan and Faye Warren," Mabel said. "Faye got a little spooked and there was an earthquake—and are you sure that you're okay?"

Jerry's lip curled. He widened the door and stepped out into the kitchen, shuffling while he walked with one foot dragging slightly. He wore a pair of plaid bed pants that were completely soaked

222

in the front by the same dark brown liquid that covered his hand.

"Faye Warren," Jerry laughed harshly. Mabel's heart skipped a beat and she followed him closely, reaching out to try and grasp his arm.

"Daddy," she pleaded. "We need to get you to a hospital. You don't look..." she couldn't tear her eyes away from the front of his pants.

"Oh, I'm gone," Jerry said. "I'm long gone, baby girl."

Faye turned, and Jerry stopped just inches away from her. Mabel flickered her gaze from one face to the other, desperately trying to decode the meaning in their silent exchange.

"I've got something that should make you happy, Ms. Warren," Jerry finally said. Faye looked him up and down and her top lip curled.

"Is it your dick on a plate?" she asked. The sound that came out of Jerry's mouth at that question was almost manic.

"Not quite, but close," he rasped. He grabbed his waistband and pushed his pants down his legs. His thighs were painted in brown slime and bright red blood. The smell that emanated from the exposed skin was like rotting fish. Mabel gagged audibly and had to stop herself from throwing up in her mouth.

"Is this what you think I deserve?" Jerry gestured with both hands down at his crotch. "It wasn't enough, what you gave me?"

"I gave you *shit*," Faye growled. Her face didn't so much as pale. If Jerry's state rattled her, it did not show on her face. "I'm not the one going around spreading shit, Jerry, that's all been you. And who the hell knows where you got it from? I don't care, but it *was not* me!"

"Who else could it have been?" Jerry almost screamed the question.

"I don't *know!* Do you think I interrogate everyone you coerce?"

"You did this to me!"

"I have a doctor who would disagree!"

Jerry turned around, his pants still around his ankles, and Mabel caught a full look at the damage. From the tops his thighs to his crotch, right where the hem of his long shirt reached, Jerry's skin was pitch black. Large blotches of discoloration, mostly purples and sickly blues, spread down towards his knees. His scrotum was grotesquely engorged, closely resembling two grocery store plums that had been pinned onto his groin. His dick was barely hanging on, looking like it was peeling away from the base, only adhered by a flap of skin and too dead to even bleed.

Mabel screamed. The shrill, ragged sound brought tears to her eyes and made her head spin. Someone put their arms around her, she suspected it was Ezra, but she could not calm herself enough to focus.

All she heard was Faye's deadpan voice, "it's always looked like that."

"Shut up!" Mabel shrieked. "Shut *up!* We need to get him to a hospital!"

224

"Mabel," Ezra whispered, hugging her close to his chest. "Shh, shh, calm down. Please."

"It's too late for me, baby girl," Jerry said. He turned around and started shuffling back towards the kitchen. Mabel watched him go by, peeking out from her place against Ezra's chest.

"No," she muttered, clinging to Ezra's shirt with her fingers wound up in the fabric. "No, he needs a doctor, daddy...!"

"Get her out of here," Jerry said. "She shouldn't be here. None of you should."

"We just drove through an earthquake," Faye said. "It was bad where we started. Who knows what the roads are like. What are you expecting us to do?"

"Find her mother," Jerry's shrug was evident in his voice. "I think she'll get more of a kick out of this."

"Let's go," Ezra whispered. Mabel tried to pull away from him.

"Ezra Buchanan, let go of me!" She screamed at the top of her lungs. Ezra released her, and Mabel staggered backwards.

"We have to *leave*," Faye said. "Your daddy wants to rot in peace."

"Faye!" Ezra sounded exasperated.

"I'm telling her the truth. I don't think anyone's ever done that before, though. She doesn't seem to know how to handle it."

Jerry disappeared back into his bedroom and shut the door behind him. The lock clicked and

Mabel ran across the kitchen. She slipped on brown residue that coated the linoleum and fell to her knees, landing hard. She caught herself on her hands and hissed in pain before continuing to crawl across the kitchen floor. She reached her father's door and smacked it with her palm, using her other hand to try and latch on to drag herself up.

"Daddy!" Mabel called out, struggling to be heard through the door. "Daddy, come out! We need to get you to a hospital!"

"He wouldn't survive the drive," Faye's voice was faint underneath all the screaming in Mabel's head. "Mabel, I swear—!"

Faye's words were cut off by a loud '*pop*' that sounded on the other side of the door, followed by a hard thump. Mabel's heart stopped and her blood ran cold, freezing everything down to the breath in her lungs.

"Jesus, no!" Unable to think, or say, anything else, Mabel just kept pounding on the door. "Jesus, no! Jesus, Jesus!"

"Mabel! Stop!" Ezra grabbed her arms and tried to pull her away from the door. Mabel thrashed and turned around to claw at him, raking her nails down Ezra's face and jamming her knee into his stomach. He went down easily, and she bolted for the front door.

"For fuck's sake, Mabel!" Faye called out. "Get back inside!"

If Faye said anything else, her words were drowned out by the sound of an oncoming train.

The sky churned above Mabel's head, and when she looked up, she saw a funnel forming on the horizon.

It was enormous. The biggest damn twister she had ever seen. At first, it didn't appear to even be moving. Mabel slowed her run, unable to stop staring.

From the main funnel, a second vortex spun off. Instead of fading out, it spiraled towards the ground, and the tornado resembled a pair of legs stalking across the horizon—like a giant.

Mabel had lost her ability to scream. Every sound she made scraped against the sides of her throat and came out as a faint, hoarse cry. The tornado looked like it was moving in place, making no progress in its journey, but the wind was whipping around her even faster, with debris from the yard hurdling across her path towards the fence.

It took her a moment to realize her face was stinging. Not only that, but when she looked at her arms, the skin looked like it was being scraped by a giant vegetable peeler, and the raw red flesh underneath was left exposed.

Mabel tried to scream, but it was a pitiful sound lost in the blaring tornado, and the twin vortexes continued their journey—dragging sheets of her skin with them.

# CHAPTER THIRTY-THRE

In the aftermath of the tornado, the dark reverend led his congregation into the streets. Some crawled over the cracks in the earth, some stepped over them, but they all stayed as close to him as possible. He led them in a hymn, and their discordant choir was the only sound that filled the eerie silence of the shell-shocked town of Sweet Providence.

When the congregation crossed the main road, all traffic stopped. An icy ball formed in Isabel's throat as she watched them pass, too big to swallow down.

Jonah was quiet, too, as they went by. She wondered if he could even register what was happening, or if the pain meds he had been given at the hospital were obscuring his perception of reality.

Given the present circumstances, she was a little bit envious if that was the case.

"What's going on?" Jonah asked. His words came out a little thick and clunky, but they were mostly coherent.

"It looks like they're doing a prayer walk or something," Isabel said. "Although I've never seen so many liquor bottles in one spot."

"Liquor bottles?" Jonah grimaced and shifted in his seat.

"That's what it looks like they're all carrying."

"Where are they going?"

"I don't know," Isabel said. "I'm not going to get out of this car to follow."

Jonah made another face and turned his head to look out the window. "Do you think Hezekiah knows yet? About Joel?"

"I'm sure that He has to," Isabel replied. "Joel didn't really have any other family, did they?"

"No," Jonah groaned. "Zee is going to kill me."

"You're being dramatic," Isabel said. "He might be angry, but He is not going to kill you."

229

"If he does, though, there's something I want you to know."

'Oh god,' Isabel thought as she flicked on her blinker. 'Here it comes.'

"I love you," Jonah said. She caught him in her peripherals, and he was looking at her again. "I would do it all again. Jerry doesn't deserve you."

Isabel bit the corner of her cheek and kept her eyes fixed on the road. "I know," she said. "I mean, no—he doesn't. And I..." it got stuck in her mouth. It wasn't like she had never waffled over the idea before, but it had always been pitting how Jonah made her feel against the *nothing* that Jerry gave her. Now she was being forced to grapple with the good Southern woman who had been raised to pleased, and the pastor's wife who was, albeit slowly, learning to stand up for herself.

There was no good answer, and the longer she let Jonah wait, the more she felt like she was suffocating.

"I love you too," she spit it out like an automatic arcade ticket at pinball machine. She glanced over at Jonah, just long enough to see the relief that was on his face.

"We could just keep going," Jonah said. "We don't have to return home. We could just...be together."

Oh, it was tempting—but far easier said than done. "I can't just abandon my family, Jonah," she said. "Mabel still lives at home and even though Jerry doesn't deserve me, he does *need* me. The whole church needs me. They would all drown if I wasn't there."

"Maybe that would be good for them," Jonah suggested softly. "Maybe they should flounder a little bit."

Isabel shook her head. "It's a nice thought," she said. "If you skipped town, I wouldn't blame you. I would miss you like hell." She took a deep breath. "But it's the way things are. We have a good thing, the two of us. But we would kill each other if we had to live in a camper van down by the river, because I don't have my own bank account and neither of us will be earning a living." With the way things were, there was comfort in the stability that the both of them *did* have. Without that, they were just two people cut adrift—and Isabel had no intention of starting over, not with a grown daughter and a mortgage.

The congregation finished crossing the road, and she hit the gas pedal.

"Does it look like they're headed towards my house?" Jonah asked.

"I don't know," Isabel told him. "But if so, I think we'll be at them there."

Isabel had never been inside the Prophet's house. It was a soft yellow, single-story building surrounded by a white fence. The front porch was overburdened by hanging potted plants, and at the end of the driveway was a carport with an old Volkswagen bus parked off to the side. She did not pull all the way underneath, opting instead to park about a foot away from the carport's shade where it was easier to pull into the yard and do a quick turnaround if she needed. She wasn't sure what she was expecting, but she liked to be prepared.

Before she even had a chance to turn off the car, the front door opened and two dogs leapt down the stairs, baying an alarm as they tore across the yard. Isabel froze as both dogs circled around the car and jumped up onto her door. They were so much taller than they looked when up on their hind legs. Their large paws thudded against her window with enough force that she was terrified the glass would break.

Jonah opened his door, and a whistle from the porch brought the dogs back across the yard. Isabel looked and saw Hezekiah standing on the steps, looking far more ghoulish underneath the ghastly, overcast sky than He ever had under the yellow church lights.

The Prophet grasped the railing that led up to His house and leaned.

"Jonah," the Prophet said. "The prodigal lover."

"I took him to the hospital," Isabel nearly jumped out of the car before Jonah had the chance to reply. "Did the police contact you about his accident...?" She realized that it wasn't just the light, Hezekiah definitely looked *worse* than usual. The dark bags underneath the Prophet's eyes looked even deeper and more purple than usual. The red around His eyes had seeped into His whites, to where it looked like He had not slept in days.

"Oh, yes," Hezekiah said. "They told me everything." Behind him, the porch door opened again, and the redheaded Amos Sleyde stepped out with his burly arms folded across his chest.

"I am sorry," Jonah choked. Isabel had never seen him in such a state before. The man folded like paper underneath the Prophet's scrutinizing gaze, his posture already wilting like he was ready to throw himself on the ground and crawl.

Something crept over her—a sort of unshakeable *ick* that she had never experienced with Jonah before.

"Lover, I don't blame you for Joel's death," Hezekiah said, His voice taking on a soft, soothing tone that Isabel had never heard before. "I do not think that it was your responsibility. I believe it was the Lord holding up a bright mirror and ripping the scales from my eyes."

"What do you mean?" Jonah asked.

Hezekiah's hands dropped down and He stroked both of His dogs behind the ears.

"The Lord sent me a vision during Babylon Prayer," Hezekiah said. "I saw Sweet Providence fall into the hands of Death, where the Lord told me that a column of fire would be the light to lead the redeemed. Of which, there will be few. So few they can be counted on a single hand, not unlike when Sodom and Gomorrah were purged for their sins." The Prophet raised His chin. "And then the Lord reminded me of a story, that of Queen Jezebel and Naboth's vineyard."

Hezekiah's words might as well have been a stone hurled towards Isabel directly. Behind His shoulder, Amos' gaze did not waver. It was bolted to her. Isabel took several steps back, glancing at Jonah, not sure what she expected from him. But *she* felt that she had to run, and had no idea why he was just staring up at the Prophet all open-mouthed and goggly-eyed.

"It seems a small problem, a strange story to tell when the end of all things is so close." Hezekiah continued. "But if Joel's death showed me anything at all, it is that the righteous will suffer if the wicked are not punished." As He talked, the dogs raised their hackles and bared their teeth, as if He had uttered some secret command.

"I am going!" Isabel announced, taking several more steps backward before daring to turn around. "I need to get home to Jerry!" Some part of her panicked logic was that if she reminded the Prophet of her connection to His preacher, he might come to His senses. Her car wasn't far away, but it felt like a mile, like she couldn't bring herself to move quickly enough.

"Zee," Jonah began, "please—"

*"And the dogs shall eat Jezebel in the portion of Jezreel, and there shall be none to bury her."* Hezekiah snarled. The dogs echoed his growl, and tags jingled as large paws struck the walkway.

Isabel's hands slammed against the side of her passenger door, groping for the handle. Her sweaty fingers refused to grip anything at all, and then pain shot up her legs and her back as nails and teeth tore into her flesh.

Isabel screamed. The weight of both dogs was too much to fight against and they dragged her to the ground. She tried to shield herself by throwing her arms into the air, but they just caught her limbs between their teeth, and blood showered down onto her face.

"Don't," Hezekiah's voice was barely audible over the growling and snapping so close to her ears. "You interfere with God's judgement."

A heavy paw bore down on her throat and Isabel choked. Teeth sank into the sides and cartilage crackled. Her whole neck went numb after that, and she could barely feel more than pressure when the teeth came down a second time.

There was still plenty of pain to go around, still. Although at some point, she lost the feeling in her legs as well.

A dark tunnel took over her vision, and she ran into its solace. No matter what waited for her on the other side, it was better than the pain, better than being torn apart by dogs.

# CHAPTER THIRTY-FOUR

Amos tried to feel pity for Isabel, but if anything, he was more upset at Hezekiah's involvement of Duke and Baron. Like everyone else, those dogs were under the heavy influence of Hezekiah's will, and they would no doubt come back more confused and upset than anything. Seeing their beautiful spotted blue coats soaked in blood wrenched his heart. All he wanted to do was grab them both and haul them into the house for a bath.

Jonah was on his knees, and he looked like he was about to throw up. Amos hated him so much.

Joel was dead, and Jonah had lived. That alone was enough to burn up what was left of Amos' already shaky faith in a higher being. If there *was* a God, He never would have let someone as precious, kind, and joyful as Joel die while insufferable leeches like Jonah continued to breathe.

Baron and Duke backed off Isabel Calhoun not long after she stopped moving. Amos called them back to his side, adding another rip to his heart when he grabbed their drenched collars.

"Zee," Amos said quietly, "I am going to take them inside."

Hezekiah waved his hand in acknowledgement.

It was only a heartbeat's length of time between that gesture and Amos straightening his back that, across the street, faces began to emerge from the tree line.

Amos' heart stopped. He looked at Hezekiah, but the prophet's expression did not change. The oncoming crowd was being led by the tallest man Amos had ever seen. In fact, he looked more like the long, thin shadow of a man that had been stretched out to unsettling proportions.

And they were all singing Gospel hymns. It took Amos only a second longer to recognize *Amazing Grace.*

"Get inside, Zee," Amos said, hauling the dogs backward to shove them into the house. He slammed the screen door shut and they jumped up against the glass, barking at the unfamiliar faces. Hezekiah shook his head.

"Death isn't something you can run from, Amos," he said. "And the redeemed need a torch to light their way."

The tall man stopped at the edge of the lawn. The front gate blew open without being touched, and the crowd began to pour in. They did not rush for Hezekiah, as Amos feared, but they filled the front yard and surrounded the porch on all sides. Jonah stood and brushed off the front of his pants, standing like he was going to take any of them on with his bare fists. Amos secretly hoped that one of them would try to hit the younger man, just to have the satisfaction of seeing him go down.

"Hezekiah Rampling," the tall man wheezed like a punctured accordion and smiled like a lipless skull. "Here we are, together. God's messengers."

"God has very different plans for you and I," Hezekiah said, straightening his posture.

"No doubt," the tall man raised his hands and spread the wide above his head, like he was welcoming the sky. "They have come to cast their sins down at your feet, in the land of reform where giants walk."

As the words left his mouth, any member of the congregation holding a liquor bottle hurled it towards the walkway. The bottles exploded as soon as they hit the pavement, spraying glass and booze onto the grass. The bottles rained down like hailstones until there was nothing left of the walkway that wasn't covered in green, brown, and clear shards. It almost looked like stained glass, from where Amos was standing.

Hezekiah held the tall man's gaze the entire time. It wasn't until the last bottle fell that he bent over and started taking off his shoes.

"Zee..." Amos started. Hezekiah cut him off with a gesture. The prophet glanced over his shoulder and gave Amos a hard look with his one good eye. Amos swallowed the rest of his protests, forcing himself to watch as Hezekiah started down the front steps, refusing to even grab onto the railing.

At the bottom of the steps, glass crunched underneath Hezekiah's bare foot. Amos winced but did not look away. More glass snapped and popped as Hezekiah took another step, and slowly, yet determinedly, the prophet continued down the walkway with his feet coated in blood and glass shards embedded into his skin.

At the end of the walkway, Hezekiah stopped only inches away from the tall man, who towered over him like a monolith. The tall man lowered his arms, just a fraction, and the ground began to tremble.

Amos grabbed onto the porch railing to keep himself upright. Some of the congregation members fell to their knees, not even trying to stay planted on their feet.

Hezekiah pulled a flask out of his pocket and unscrewed the cap, flipping the top off and emptying it over his head. It did not smell like alcohol, from where Amos was standing. It smelled like lighter fluid.

"Zee!" He screamed, gripping the porch railing until his knuckles turned white. "Hezekiah! Don't!"

Hezekiah's fingers flicked open a lighter, just enough to produce a pale, barely visible flame.

The flame became a blaze as it caught Hezekiah's sleeve, and then a conflagration as it consumed the prophet's entire body.

"Behold, the Flaming Chariot!" orange flames cast hellish light onto the tall man's face as he cried out. His words were barely heard above Hezekiah's screams.

The congregation echoed Hezekiah's cries, tearing at their hair and clothes, rending themselves to pieces, throwing themselves onto the ground. The trembling had already stopped, but Amos had not even noticed.

Panic gripped Amos' broad chest and made his head spin. He could barely think. All he could see was Hezekiah's skin peeling, burning, and the flames licking at his suit jacket, eating it away from his shoulders.

"Jonah!" Amos screamed. "Get the hose! Hose him down!"

Jonah looked around, his eyes wide, flashing white like a scared horse. "Where is it?" Jonah threw himself down into the mulch and started digging. "Where is it? *Where is it?*"

"Fucking Christ, you useless fucking bastard!" Amos barreled down the stairs and grabbed the hose from its hook near the side of the house. He did not waste time unraveling the entire thing before twisting the nozzle and unleashing a harsh jet onto Hezekiah's burning body. The prophet screamed even louder when the cold water hit him. The congregation echoed those screams, as well, writhing on the ground like it was their own bodies being burned.

Even with Hezekiah being doused, Amos was too late to save the yard. The grass had already caught fire, and the flames were spreading towards the people clustered together inside the fence. It caught on pant legs and skirts and spread upward from there, until every squirming, thrashing body was on fire. Their screams were swallowed up by columns of foul-smelling smoke, and the flames were carried by the wind, throwing it upward into twisting vortexes like a Biblical column of fire.

The tall man had not moved. Amos abandoned the hose and went to grab Hezekiah's soaked body. His lover badly burned, but still breathing. Amos pulled off Hezekiah's soaked jacket to lighten the load just a little before lifting him into the air.

From the trees came a flurry of black wings, vultures so large that they shook the boughs when they launched themselves into the air. The man at the end of the walkway turned his face towards the sky, and his grey skin flushed red.

"And from the ruins, the dead in Christ shall rise—and rise, and rise!" His face transformed. His prominent nose hooked and fused with his shriveled mouth until it formed something closer to a beak. Black wings sprang from between his shoulder-blades and spread out, spanning twice the length of the house. Horror kept Amos rooted to his spot, but only for a moment. Having Hezekiah in his arms was enough to start him running.

Amos sprinted across the yard. He reached out one hand and grabbed Jonah by the collar as he went by, half-dragging the younger man with him as he ran. Jonah stumbled while trying to stay upright and attempted to wrestle himself out of Amos' grip.

Amos just held onto him tighter.

"Don't make me drop you, or him," Amos snarled. "I will leave you to the vultures. Get into the van." The Volkswagen had a problem with its alignment, which was why he hadn't driven it, but he would be damned if he let that keep him from taking Hezekiah to a proper hospital.

Amos opened up the van doors and threw Jonah inside. Once Jonah had found a seat, more or less, Amos passed Hezekiah to him.

"I am going to get Duke and Baron. *Stay here,*" Amos warned. He pinned Jonah down with a glare, just to make sure the younger man knew he meant it, and then went back to the house—gunning for the side door.

Duke and Baron came running to him as soon as he was inside, terrified by all the screaming and the smoke. He grabbed them by their collars and pulled them outside. They fought him, but he kept pulling, too determined to get them to safety to feel guilty about his method of extraction. His arms and lungs burned, but he could not falter, not now.

Amos got the dogs out to the van, letting them climb in on their own before slamming the door shut. He hopped into the driver's seat, the entire process feeling like hours, but in reality was only minutes.

"What if we can't get out?" Jonah asked.

"Shut up," Amos said. "I don't want to hear a word from you, so *shut up.*" He caught a glimpse of Hezekiah's burned face in his rearview mirror, and then he revved up the engine.

When Amos came peeling out from underneath the carport, the sky was black with vultures.

# CHAPTER THIRTY-FIVE

**M**abel Calhoun's body was completely unrecognizable as anything other than a pile of raw, jumbled limbs piled in her yard. Her skin had been ripped clean off by the wind and sand, and to Ezra, she looked more like the pork bones he bought for Winston than a human being any longer.

Faye touched his arm. Ezra put his hand on top of hers and squeezed her fingers.

"I'm sorry, babe," Faye said.

Ezra swallowed hard and shook his head. "It doesn't feel real," he said. "Any of it. Nothing about today feels like it really happened."

"I know," Faye rubbed his arm as she spoke. She then prompted him, gently, wordlessly, to take his crutch and he did so.

"We should get going," Faye said. "We can't just stand around here."

"The sky still looks ugly," Ezra said. "Maybe we should stay put until it's completely clear."

"Or end up like that," Faye pointed at Mabel's mangled body. "I don't know if I want to continue taking cover in a house with a dead preacher in the bathroom."

Ezra made a face and nodded. The yard was a mess, and his car was nowhere to be seen. "We're going to have to walk," he said. He hated that thought, but they had no other choice.

"I'll follow your lead," Faye told him. She looked towards the horizon and cupped her hand over her brow. "Look at that." She pointed, and Ezra followed the line of her gesture. Against the sky, towering above a faint line of trees, there was an ugly, billowing column of smoke.

Underneath the howling wind, he could also hear screams.

"We can double back," Ezra said, "if the storm has moved that way. We should be safe going back where we came from."

"Something worse than the storm might be that way," Faye remarked.

"Maybe," Ezra said. "Do you have a better idea?"

Faye shrugged. She did not. Ezra gripped his crutch and started walking back the way they came, trying his best not to look too hard at Mabel's body as they passed.

# CHAPTER THIRTY-SIX

On all sides, Sweet Providence was being torn apart. Where the earth was divided, entire buildings were starting to slide into the cracks. Vehicles with smoking engines and blaring horns were lodged in tangled treetops and the roads nearly inaccessible, some of them in such disrepair that the asphalt had become dislodged and started creating cliff-like structures.

The strangest thing about it all was there was no panic. The roads were eerily devoid of people. The few that Amos could see were crawling on their bellies, wriggling through the dry grass like snakes and slithering into the giant cracks. There were plenty of dead bodies, too, most of them covered head-to-toe in vultures—many stripped down to nothing but bone.

Amos drove as carefully as he could. It was hard not to start catastrophizing about whether there was even a hospital still waiting for them at the end of the line. Was the damage only in Sweet Providence, or had it extended even farther out? What was he going to do, if he could not get Hezekiah taken care of?

His lover had fallen asleep in the backseat. Jonah was staring out a window, watching the horrific scene with all the vacant expression of someone scrolling through daytime television. Amos ground his teeth so hard that they squealed in his ear, and did not let up until they had passed the painted wooden sign at the city limits. 'WELCOME TO SWEET PROVIDENCE! EST. 1809."

Duke and Baron laid on top of and underneath Hezekiah, doing their part to nurse him back to health. They were Amos' only comfort. The only ones he could rely on anymore.

Past the city limits, it was nothing but forest and fields on either side. The roads began to even out, and Amos regained some of his confidence in their ability to find help. He tried not to get his hopes up too high. He drove for about twenty minutes, glancing in the rearview mirror every few seconds just to see whether Hezekiah was still breathing.

Finally, he stuck his tongue between his teeth and turned off his lights. He pulled the van over to the side of the road and parked in a thick section of bushes, deep enough to obscure the entire front half.

He didn't turn off the car, but he did turn around in his seat and look at Jonah.

"Get out," he said.

"Why?" Jonah gave him a questioning look. "Need someone to watch you piss?"

"Get. Out." Amos growled. "I need to talk to you."

Jonah's eyebrows went up, but he complied. He crawled over the seat, over Hezekiah, and let himself out the door. Amos stepped out also, loosening his belt and whipping it free from its loops as he circled the back of the van.

By the time he reached Jonah, he had it doubled over in his hand.

He *shouldn't* do it. Amos wasn't the type of man who ever wanted to hurt anybody. He had long ago learned to channel his anger through more productive avenues than physical aggression. But *now*...it was more than anger. It was deeper than that. This was *Jonah,* the little pissant who couldn't even find a garden hose to stop Hezekiah from burning to death. The same asshole who could never be bothered to clean out his car, or do dishes, or keep his dick in his pants.

250

The same *bastard* who had to be practically held at gunpoint to take Joel to the hospital, and had been driving his *piece of shit* car so irresponsibly that now, Joel was dead.

Hezekiah was in agony, and Jonah had done nothing to stop it.

Jonah. *Jonah.* Worthless. Rubbish. *Waste of skin and semen.*

Amos struck Jonah across the back of the neck with the belt. Jonah yelped and whipped around, but Amos hit him again before he could retaliate. The second and third blows struck Jonah on the face and arm, and then every blow after that struck him on the torso, the back, and the head. Jonah might have been taller, but Amos was stronger, and Jonah went reeling back on his narrow legs until he toppled to the crowd. The younger man was shouting, but Amos wasn't listening. He had no interest in anything coming out of that piece of shit's mouth.

Jonah tried to flip himself over onto his stomach to crawl, and Amos stepped on his hands. He stomped as hard as he could on Jonah's knuckles until he heard things start to snap. Jonah's screams sent birds scattering into the air from their roosts. Strangely, inside the van, the dogs were silent.

Amos stood after being doubled over from beating the hell out of the younger man. His movement granted Jonah only a few seconds of reprieve before he planted his boot in the dead center of the younger man's chest. Amos wrapped his belt around Jonah's neck, pulling it so tight that it dug into the white, freckled skin and drained it of all its color before turning it blue. Jonah's eyes bulged and he choked, clawing at the belt around his neck with his mangled fingers. Amos gripped the belt, wrapping it around his head and hauling Jonah's head up enough to punch him directly in the nose.

Blood exploded across Jonah's face, and he stopped sputtering. Satisfied, Amos kept his grip on the belt and dragged Jonah across the ground. It was a short distance, but still long enough to be uncomfortable with rocks and brambles stabbing at every inch of exposed skin. Amos stopped at the nearest tree and hauled Jonah up, throwing him against the trunk and holding him there while he struggled to loop the other end of the belt around the lowest branch.

Jonah laughed at him, a nasty wet sound with all the blood running down his nose and throat.

"That's not going to kill me," he said. Amos tightened the belt around its branch and Jonah winced. The belt pulled his head up at a sharp, uncomfortable angle, digging into the soft part of his chin while cutting off his breathing.

"Not quickly," Amos hissed in his ear. He pulled back, only marginally satisfied with his work. Even with broken hands, there was a chance that Jonah could wriggle free from the belt. The branch could break, or someone could find him and cut him down. Nothing was impossible.

Amos reached into his jeans and pulled out his favorite pocketknife. He'd had it since he was sixteen, and he carried it everywhere. Without saying a word, he grabbed Jonah's shirt cut a notch, using that to rip the fabric apart and tear the whole garment off.

Once Jonah's chest was bare, Amos grabbed the younger man's red curls and wrenched his head so that their gazes were locked. Jonah's face was turning purple from the awkward angle, with blood and bubbles of clear spittle forming at the corners of his bruised mouth.

Amos looked him in the eye and plunged his knife into Jonah's side. The man screamed and blood ran down the blade, coating the handle, but Amos did not lose his grip. He drew the knife along the wall of Jonah's abdomen, opening his belly in a gaping, ghoulish grin that vomited entrails onto the ground.

Jonah's body twitched like a fish on a line. Amos wrapped his knife up in the shredded shirt and wiped as much blood off his hands as he could. He didn't spare Jonah another glance. He was not interested in the man's fate any longer. Let the vultures eat him, or the coyotes, or whatever else found him first.

Amos walked back to the van and got back into the driver's seat. He glanced in the rearview mirror to watch Hezekiah's chest rise and fall a few times before turning the headlights back on.

"Is everything all right back there?" He asked. Duke and Baron stared back at him, but he felt their silent approval in their wagging tails.

Amos backed out onto the road and hit the gas. He had wasted a lot of time, but now he could at least put his focus back onto Hezekiah, without Jonah sitting there—wasting air.

# CHAPTER THIRTY-SEVEN

Ezra's legs burned, and by his desperate gesture, Faye stopped walking so he could catch up. By the time he reached her, his face was hot and his head was reeling. They had not even been walking very long, but his spine was screaming.

"Come here," Faye directed him to sit. Ezra plopped down into the grass, the impact making him wince, and lowered his crutch down beside him. Faye sat down as well, close enough that she could touch her knee to his. Ezra stayed upright for as long as he could and then lowered himself down onto his back.

"We're going to die here," he said.

"No," she countered. "We're not going to die."

"We haven't seen anyone else," Ezra said. "Have you noticed that? Isn't that odd, to you?"

"I don't know. I've been so relieved that I hardly noticed." Faye pushed her fingers through his hair, playing with the strands. "We're close, you know."

"Close to what?" He asked.

"The revival tent," she said. "It's just up there."

"Goodie," he sighed. "But you can't see anyone?"

"No," she told him. "Doesn't mean that no one is there."

"True," Ezra pulled himself back up, grimacing at the pain that shot up towards his skull. "Should we go inside?"

"Why would we?" She asked. "To see if someone will help us? I don't know if anyone is still alive."

"I don't know," Ezra said. "But I can't think of anything better."

Faye pondered it for a minute, then she shrugged. She stood, brushing off the grass from her pants, and then held out her hand to help him up. Once Ezra was back on his feet, he hobbled after her towards the giant white revival tent.

The tent was as empty as he had ever seen it. The dead tree that loomed near the entrance was devoid of any occupants, but there were plenty of black feathers littering the ground underneath. Ezra and Faye exchanged a look and they moved a little closer. She reached out to grab a flap and pulled it back, gesturing for him to walk in.

"After you," she said.

Ezra rolled his eyes and stepped inside. He had not even realized how oppressive the post-storm humidity was until he was hit in the face with crisp, cool air. Ezra took a deep breath and kept moving, glancing around at the orderly rows of aluminum chairs that looked like they had not been touched once.

"It's like we were never here," Faye said, and her voice carried and undercurrent of awe. Ezra nodded his agreement, his own heart racing at a thousand miles a minute.

At the end of the row that pulpit still stood, as tall and as red as ever. Ezra stopped in front of it and stood there, staring at his face in the burnished brass cross.

Another face appeared behind his, sunken and warped by the metal.

"Do you know what it is, to be redeemed?" The voice of Reverend Grievance asked. Ezra's heart plummeted and he spun around, gripping his crutch, prepared to wield it like a baseball bat if he needed to. Faye was right beside him, frozen in her place. Her eyes were wide, and he could see her pulse jump in her throat.

"I didn't come here for redemption," Ezra said, swallowing all his fear to get the words out. The reverend stood in front of him, hands tucked behind his back, scrawny neck bent just so that his head looked a little too heavy.

"Perhaps not," Grievance swiveled his attention to Faye. "But you did."

"I did," Faye agreed softly. "But I don't think that I know what redemption even means, anymore."

"It means nothing," Grievance said. "Redemption is a word used by the pious to rake in worldly goods from the devout." He made an odd, popping noise with his tongue. "We are pack animals, us heralds of death. And when we've picked the bones of this sinful den clean, we will move on to the next. What will become of you?"

"Shouldn't we be asking you that?" Ezra wondered aloud. "We aren't the only ones left alive, are we?"

Grievance smiled, but didn't answer.

"If you aren't going to help us, we're going to leave," Faye said, breaking free from her trance to take a determined step forward.

Grievance held up one hand. "I am not here to help," he said. "One of you must help *me*."

"To do what?" Ezra asked. "And why should we?"

Grievance closed his hand and lowered it. When he opened it again, an open penknife with a slim, delicate blade rested across his palm.

"I have worn this face for almost a century," the reverend said. "It is wearing thin. I need a new one to continue my work. To punish the sinners. To reap their souls. One of you will see eternity through my eyes. Every secret of this universe and beyond, of God and angels and the devil himself will be yours to know."

Ezra swallowed hard. He looked at Faye, but he found no answer in her eyes.

"You want a face?" Ezra's voice faltered. "What if neither of us gives you one?"

Grievance shrugged. There was no real answer. No consequence. There was no need for a punishment, when the potential reward was so great.

"How do you take it?" Faye finally asked.

"A simple incision," Grievance said. "You will not feel it. Like many things, it is painless if you do not dwell on the act."

They stood there, all three, in silence for what felt like hours. Reverend Grievance was perfectly still, balancing the knife on his outstretched palm. He might as well have been made of stone.

"I don't know," Faye said, breaking the silence.

"What happens to her, if I do it?" Ezra asked.

Again, there was no answer. Ezra reached out and took Faye's hand in his.

"It is not as if either of us has been very happy," Ezra said slowly.

"Only with each other," Faye gave him a small smile. "And even then..."

"Have you decided?" the reverend asked. His lavender eyes were pricks of unbearably bright light buried in the caverns of his sockets.

Ezra and Faye both turned towards him, and they squeezed each other's hands.

"I think so."

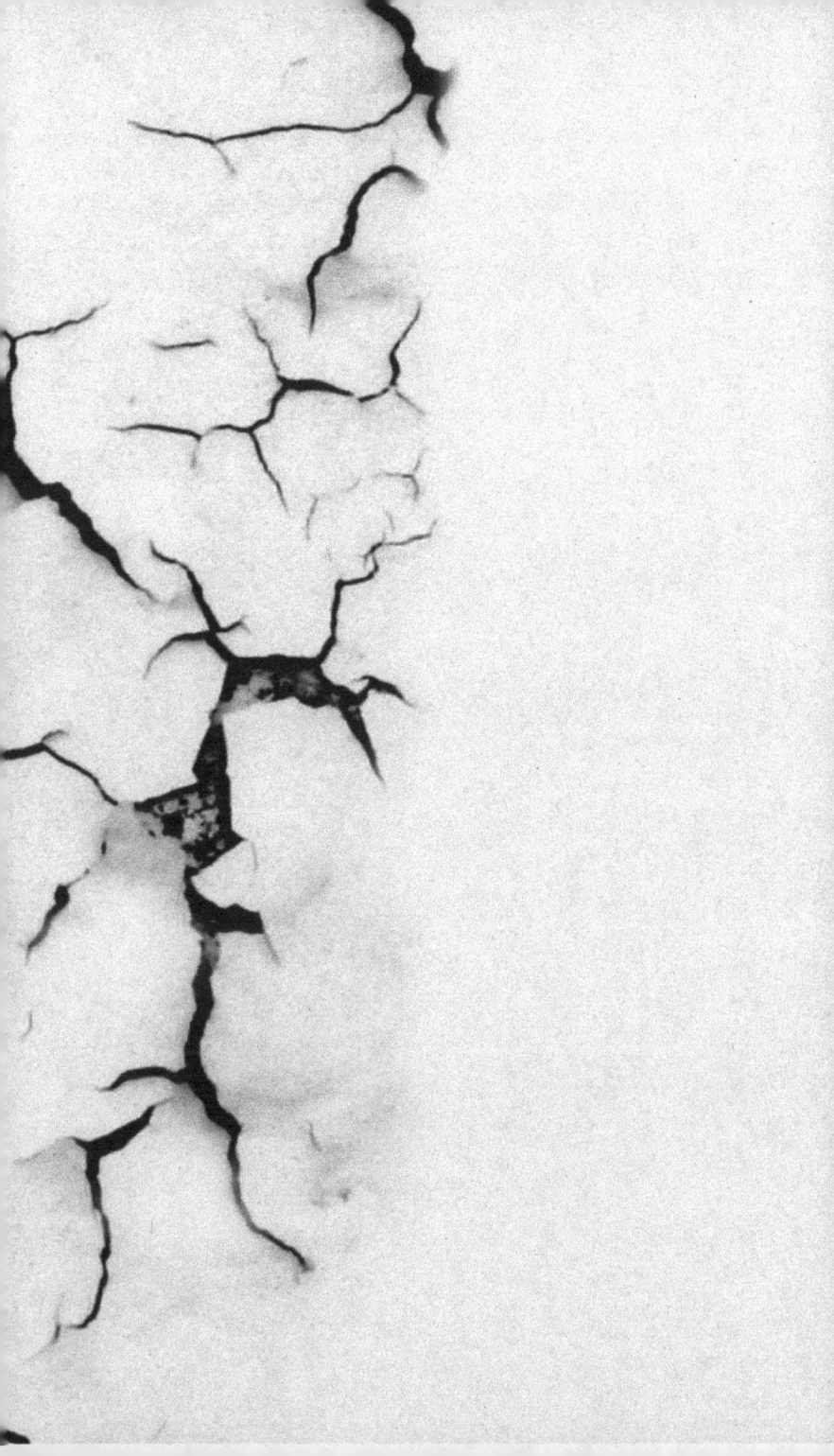

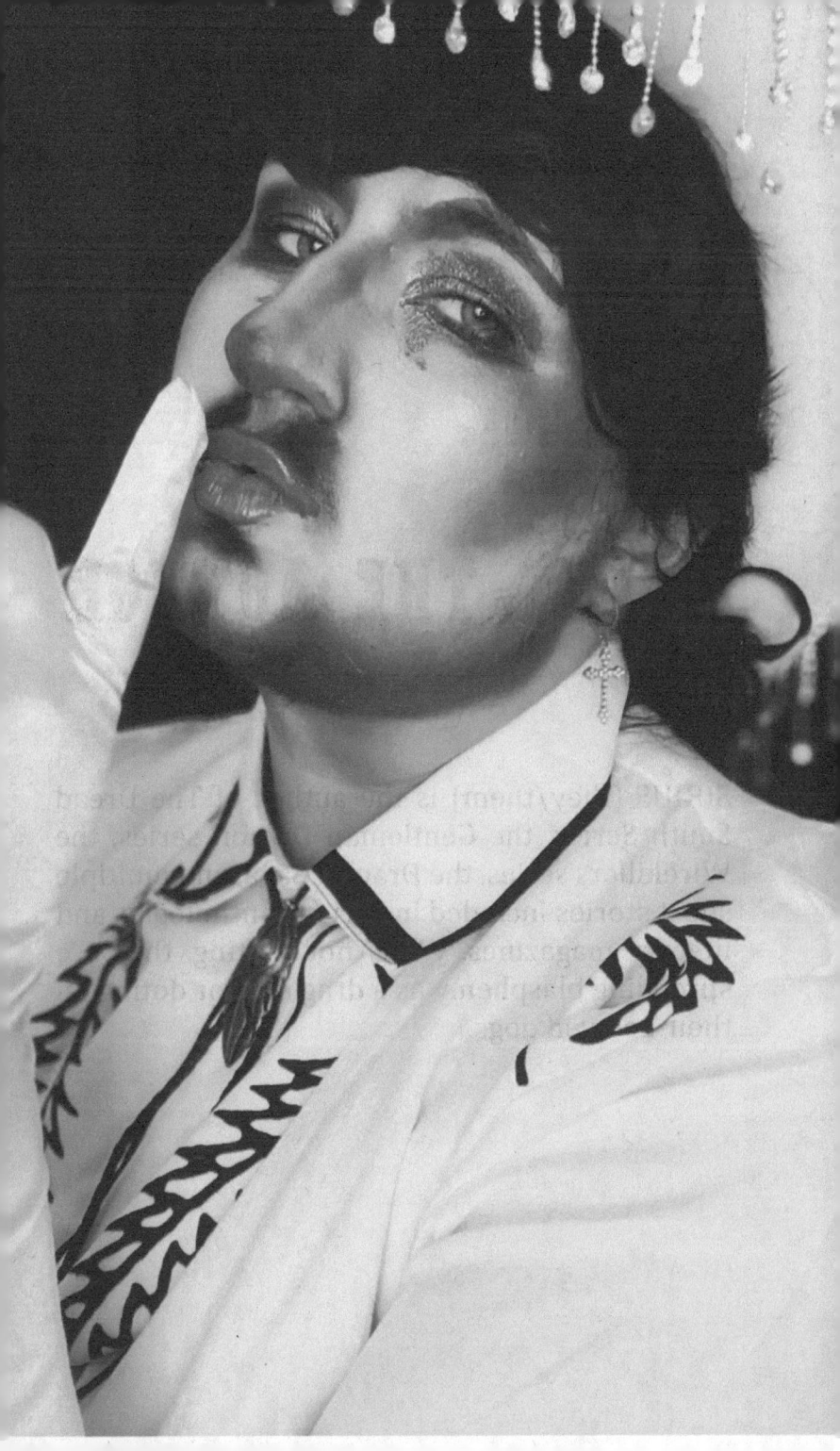

# ABOUT THE AUTHOR

SIRIUS (they/them) is the author of The Dread South Series, the Gentleman Demon series, the Wirekillers series, the Draonir Saga, and multiple short stories included in various anthologies and literary magazines. When not writing, they are spreading blasphemy as a drag king or doting on their beloved dogs.

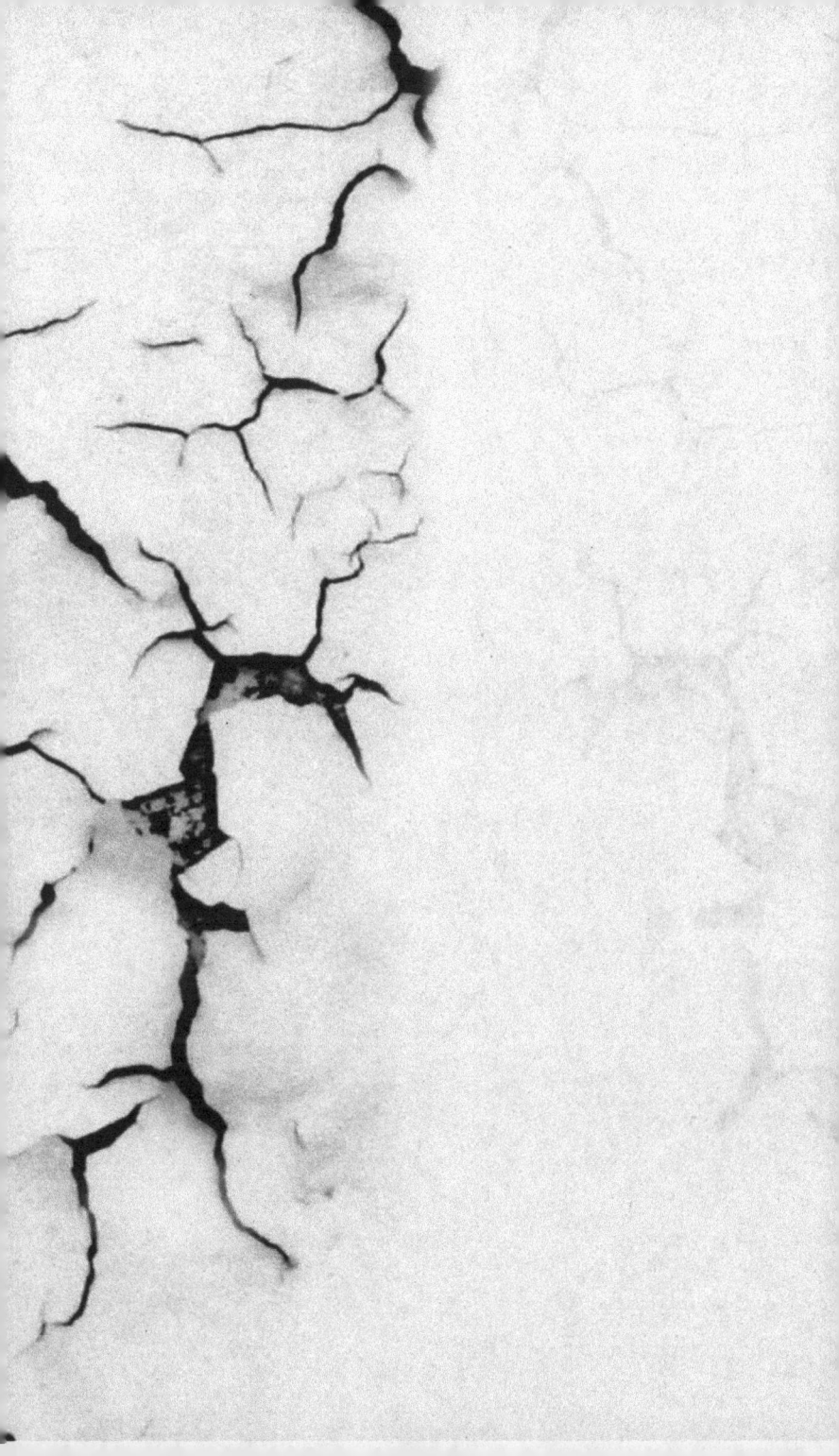

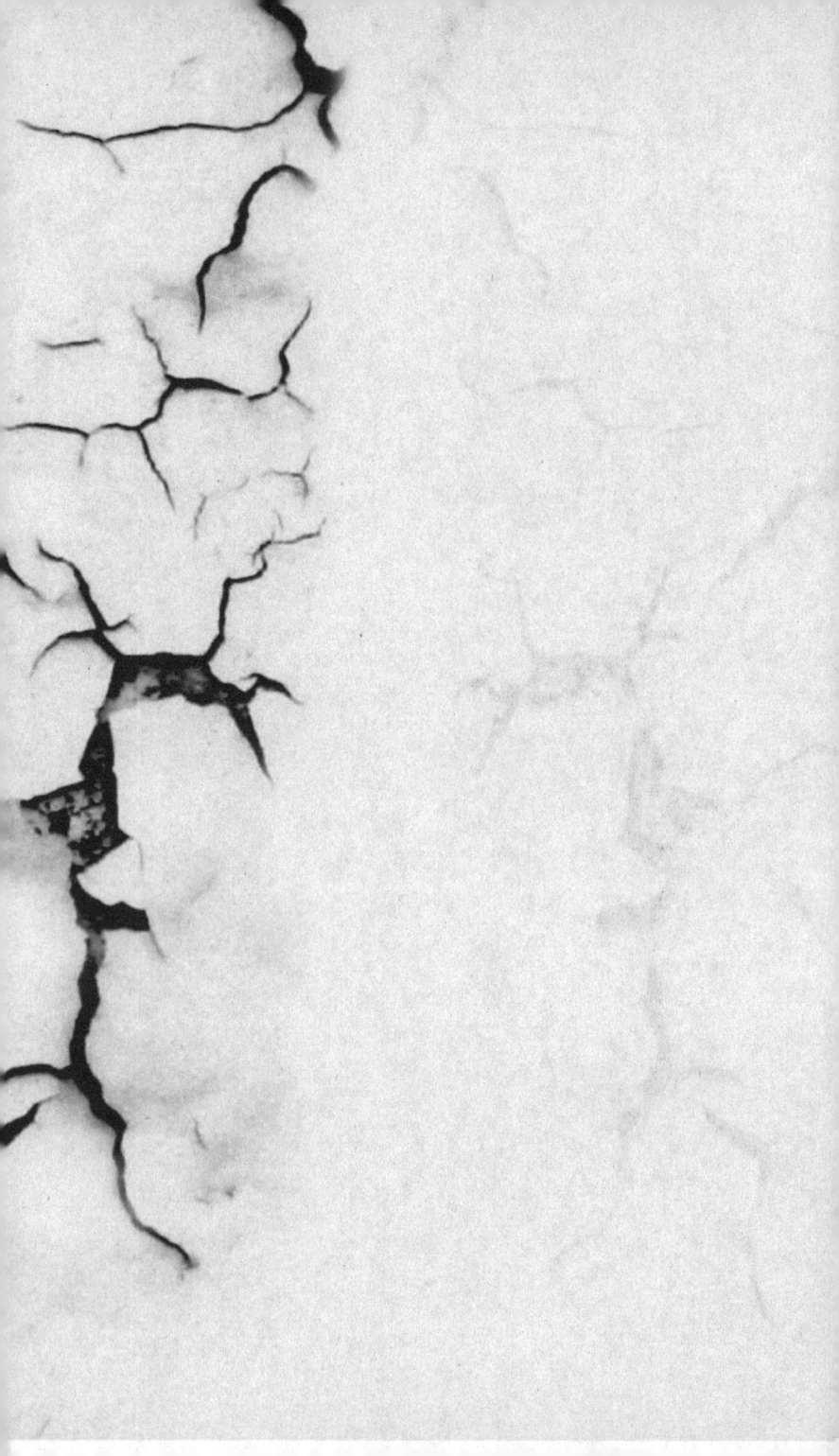

www.ingramcontent.com/pod-product-compliance
Lightning Source LLC
Chambersburg PA
CBHW011916130726
47903CB00016B/3046